Dreamland (or a musical riff on Shakespeare's *Midsummer* set during the declassification of Area 51)

Music & Book by Chris Miller

Book & Lyrics by Nathan Tysen

CONCORD
THEATRICALS

CONCORDTHEATRICALS.COM   CONCORDTHEATRICALS.CO.UK

FOR PRODUCTION ENQUIRIES

UNITED STATES AND CANADA
info@concordtheatricals.com
1-866-979-0447

UNITED KINGDOM AND EUROPE
licensing@concordtheatricals.co.uk
020-7054-7200

Each title is subject to availability from Concord Theatricals Corp., depending upon country of performance. Please be aware that *DREAMLAND* may not be licensed by Concord Theatricals Corp. in your territory. Professional and amateur producers should contact the nearest Concord Theatricals Corp. office or licensing partner to verify availability.

publisher. No one shall upload this title(s), or part of this title(s), to any social media websites.

For all enquiries regarding motion picture, television, and other media rights, please contact Concord Theatricals Corp.

MUSIC USE NOTE

Licensees are solely responsible for obtaining formal written permission from copyright owners to use copyrighted music in the performance of this play and are strongly cautioned to do so. If no such permission is obtained by the licensee, then the licensee must use only original music that the licensee owns and controls. Licensees are solely responsible and liable for all music clearances and shall indemnify the copyright owners of the play(s) and their licensing agent, Concord Theatricals Corp., against any costs, expenses, losses and liabilities arising from the use of music by licensees. Please contact the appropriate music licensing authority in your territory for the rights to any incidental music.

IMPORTANT BILLING AND CREDIT REQUIREMENTS

If you have obtained performance rights to this title, please refer to your licensing agreement for important billing and credit requirements.

DREAMLAND was commissioned by the Educational Theatre Association and presented in a staged reading, sponsored by Concord Theatricals, as part of the Thespian Musicalworks program at the 2019 International Thespian Festival in Lincoln, Nebraska on June 29, 2019. The production was directed by Nathan Tysen, with music direction by Nils-Petter Ankarblom. The stage manager was Grace Coil, with assistance from Zachary Holzberg. Jesse Wilen served as audio technician. The cast was as follows:

MELISSA SIMMS . . . . Kasey Murphy

COLONEL RASMUSSON . . . . Jose Perez

PRINCIPAL WILSON . . . . Bryanna Martinez

SNYDER . . . . .Harrison Lewis

CAMERA OPERATOR . . . . .Zachary Holzbert

REBECCA . . . . .Jessie Rathbun

RANDY . . . . Edin Inestroza

ELIOT . . . . .Dominic DeCicco

AURORA. . . . . Sarah Charles Lewis

QUINN . . . . .Ann-Terese Arreyako

SCOTT. . . . . Caden Large

OBERON . . . . Munachimso Mbaezue

TITANIA . . . . .Ashley Jackson

PUCK . . . . .Hannah Main

COBWEB . . . . Hayley Johnson

PEASEBLOSSOM. . . . . .Brianna Roberts

ENSEMBLE (SHOW CHOIR & ALIENS) . . . .
   Tatiana Arias, Samantha Belinski, Lucca Benigni, Philip Seth Bondi, Austin Brown, Alpha Camara, Kathryn Gilbride, Amelia Hoffman, Elena Holder, MacKenzie Hornak, Robyn Kerachsky, James Lammers, Noah Manzanares, Jack Morrill, Kandy Otchere-Boakye, Ricky Powers, Luke Ray Reilly, Cara-Hope Tomlinson

DREAMLAND subsequently received its world premiere at Salina South High School in Salina, Kansas on January 30, 2020. The production was directed by Kate Lindsay, with music direction by Eddie B. Creer Jr., pit conducting by Alyssa Lane, lighting design by J.R. Lidgett, scenic design by Josh Morris, choreography by Sam DeChant, and costume design by Kay Engelland, Pam Debold, and Eve Boyle. The stage managers were Alyssa Peppers, Cameron Post, and Yesenia Torres, with assistance from Ethen Lainer and Reese Kimmi. The cast was as follows:

MELISSA SIMMS . . . . .Holly Johnson

COLONEL RASMUSSON . . . . Hunter Dunshie

PRINCIPAL WILSON . . . . Maisy Lowers

SNYDER . . . . .Santiago Vasquez

CAMERA OPERATOR . . . . .Melissa Lidgett

REBECCA . . . . Whitney Turner

RANDY . . . . Nathan Streeter

ELIOT . . . . .Jacob Sweet

AURORA. . . . . Courtney White

QUINN . . . . Lauren Zimmerman

SCOTT. . . . . .Aidan Heusman

OBERON . . . . .Gavin Jones

TITANIA . . . . .Amaya Dungan

PUCK . . . . .Ashley Carraway

COBWEB . . . . .Maddy Turner

PEASEBLOSSOM. . . . . .Allison Hull

SHOW CHOIR . . . . Savannah Bonilla, Evan Dickson, Kaydence Dickson, Thomas Flores, Diana Geist, Casey Grennan, Michael Hauser, Dawson Jamison, Layla Jordan, Thomas Moyer, Addie Ollenberger, Joey Priester, Andrew Schrage, Addy Sheridan, Chantal Torres, Ellias Torres

ALIENS . . . . Kylie Bathon, Kinzie Clark, Nate Cosco, Mia Dennett, Ryan Graff, Jalyn Gutierrez, Andrew Lagerman, De'Nisha Magee, Aubrey Powell, Sarah Schrage, Ivan Solis, Shelby Stolzenburg, Molly Temple

CHARACTERS

ADULTS

MELISSA SIMMS – Channel 9 news reporter. Excellent in front of the camera, and a force to be reckoned with away from it.

COLONEL RASMUSSON – High ranking officer of the Air Force, and government liaison for Dreamland. Imposing, but gregarious, convinced his facility has nothing to hide.

PRINCIPAL WILSON – Principal of Las Vegas Prep School. The only chaperone for the weekend, so a bit jumpy. Parent of Rebecca. Can be any gender.

SNYDER – The last of a long line of caretakers at Area 51. Dreams of being an entertainer.

CAMERA OPERATOR – Employee of Channel 9 News. A person of few words. Can be any gender.

HONOR STUDENTS

REBECCA – Teenage pilot. Dreams of joining the Air Force. Leader of the honor students and daughter of Principal Wilson.

RANDY – Lover of geology, radiobiology, and Rebecca.

ELIOT – Meteorology enthusiast who dreams of being a TV weatherman and going on a date with Rebecca.

AURORA – Astronomy buff and secret conspiracy theorist who believes in alien life. Has severe social anxiety, and is misunderstood because of it.

SHOW CHOIR

NEW DAWN – Show choir at Las Vegas Prep School comprised of energetic and eager triple threats. Flexible size.

QUINN – Student elected director/choreographer of New Dawn. Can be any gender.

SCOTT – New Dawn's resident student composer.

ALIENS

ALIENS – Extraterrestrials who have been stranded on Earth for over sixty years. Obsessed with the music of the 1950s. Flexible size.

OBERON – Co-captain of the alien expedition, determined to return home. Can be any gender.

TITANIA – Co-captain of the alien expedition, no-nonsense.

PUCK - Youngest member of the expedition, a troublemaker. Can be any gender.

COBWEB, PEASEBLOSSOM, MOTH & MUSTARDSEED – Minions of Titania.

SETTING

Groom Lake Air Force Base, Hiko, Nevada; sometimes referred to as Area 51.

TIME

Now.

AUTHORS' NOTE

A few things to keep in mind: the show is a fast-paced B-movie send-up of *A Midsummer Night's Dream*, silly and a little outrageous. Depending on the size of your cast, it is possible for the show choir and the aliens to be played by the same group of actors, provided their costumes are easily swapped. These two groups perform the big production numbers, of which there are quite a few; think *Glee* on crack. Designers should not be afraid to embrace a creative, low-tech/low-budget approach to the set and costumes. While a realistic bunker/hangar can be very effective, the whole show could be done on a set of scaffolding; furthermore, a 2-D tinfoil and cardboard rocket ship could prove just as effective as a 3-D metallic one if the actors imbue it with authenticity. As noted, many characters can be cast in any gender, just swap pronouns.

SONG LIST

ACT I

"Action News Jingle" .... **FEMALE ENSEMBLE**

"New Dawn" .... **NEW DAWN**

"Lab Intro / Underscore" .... **LAB STUDENTS**

"New Dawn Ending" .... **NEW DAWN**

"Follow the Stars" .... **AURORA**

"Weatherman" .... **ELIOT**

"Follow the Stars (Reprise)" ...... **AURORA, ELLIOT, REBECCA & RANDY**

"Area 51" .... **NEW DAWN**

"Area 51 (Redacted)" .... **BEVERLY, SAM, KELLY, ADAM**

"Show Me the Stage" .... **SNYDER & NEW DAWN**

"Until the Day" .... **ALIENS**

"Until the Day (Reprise)" .... **ALIENS**

"Two Steps Ahead" .... **PUCK, MOTH & MUSTARDSEED**

"Aurora" .... **ELIOT, RANDY & ALIENS**

"23,360" .... **OBERON, TITANIA & ALIENS**

"Dreamland" .... **REBECCA, ELIOT, RANDY & AURORA**

ACT II

"Totally Safe" .... **NEW DAWN & SYNDER**

"Aurora (Reprise)" .... **TITANIA & NEW DAWN**

"Kodiak" ..... **RANDY, MOTH, MUSTARDSEED, ELIOT & OFFSTAGE VOICES**

"Sweet Dreams" .... **TITANIA, COBWEB & PEASEBLOSSOM**

"Aurora (Reprise) / Contact" ...... **AURORA, PUCK & OFFSTAGE VOICES**

"Action News Jingle (Reprise)" .... **FEMALE ENSEMBE**

"Last Day on Earth" .... **NEW DAWN**

"Finale" .... **NEW DAWN**

ACT I

Scene One

(In the darkness we hear:)

[MUSIC NO. 01 "ACTION NEWS JINGLE"]

VOICEOVER (FEMALE ENSEMBLE).
ACTION NEWS. CHANNEL 9 NEWS
ACTION! ACTION! SO MUCH ACTION!
ACTION NEWS. CHANNEL 9 NEWS
MELISSA SIMMS REPORTING LIVE!

(Lights rise on a large military hangar. A small film crew is taping a segment.)

CAMERA OPERATOR. In five, four, three, (two, one)...

MELISSA. Area 51. Top secret military facility. For decades the government refused to even acknowledge its existence. But not anymore. In a thrilling turn of events, the United States Air Force has decided to declassify this base and open it to the public. I'm here with Colonel Rasmusson. Colonel, are you really saying there is nothing to hide at Area 51?

RASMUSSON. Let's start by calling this place by its proper name: Dreamland. There is no facility called Area 51, those are simply grid coordinates on a map.

MELISSA. Dreamland? Really?

RASMUSSON. It's the radio callsign pilots use for this restricted airspace, and the perfect name for this family friendly attraction, just a hundred miles north of Las Vegas.

MELISSA. The question on everyone's mind, are there any aliens at this facility?

> *(During the next exchange, something with an extremely large head appears far upstage and slowly crosses toward them. They never see it.)*

RASMUSSON. No. No aliens. No extraterrestrials. No little green men. They are not here, and never have been. In a gesture of total transparency, we think it is important to open our doors so Americans can see first-hand how this formerly top-secret facility was run.

MELISSA. And to be clear, you are saying there are no aliens.

RASMUSSON. Not even in the gift shop. I've been saying it for thirty years, and I will say it until I'm blue in the face. There are no aliens at this facility.

> *(**MELISSA** turns to see a **GIANT ALIEN** behind them. She screams! **RASMUSSON** pulls out a walkie talkie.)*

Code 15! Code 15! We've got a code 15!

> *(Before **RASMUSSON** can subdue the **ALIEN**, the **ALIEN** pulls off his head, revealing **SCOTT**, an eager teenager.)*

SCOTT. Hi! I'm Scott. Composer lyricist singer dancer actor and occasional mask-maker. Also student director of Las Vegas Prep School's twelve-time state champion show choir.

RASMUSSON. *(Into his walkie talkie.)* Abort. I repeat abort. *(To **SCOTT**.)* You, son, are also lucky to be alive.

> *(**PRINCIPAL WILSON** enters, followed by a high school show choir wearing matching show jackets and rehearsal clothes. They are led by **QUINN**, the student choreographer.)*

PRINCIPAL WILSON. Scott! Scott! Back with the others please.

QUINN. Let's get into positions everyone!

*(**NEW DAWN** starts to warm-up, stretching and going over dance combinations.)*

PRINCIPAL WILSON. Hi, sorry about that. I'm Principal Wilson of Las Vegas Prep School.

RASMUSSON. Of course. Welcome. All of you. And congratulations. *(To **MELISSA**.)* These students are the first civilians to ever step foot on this base.

MELISSA. Principal Wilson, how does it feel to have your school selected for such an honor?

PRINCIPAL WILSON. It's a once in a lifetime opportunity, and our show choir is thrilled to share the musical theater piece they've created about Area 51 –

RASMUSSON. Dreamland!

PRINCIPAL WILSON. – Dreamland. Sorry.

[MUSIC NO. 02 "NEW DAWN"]

*(An epic music fanfare starts. **NEW DAWN** strikes a pose.)*

MELISSA. Oh, are they performing now?

*(The **SHOW CHOIR** unfreezes and starts to dance. She turns to stop them.)*

The show isn't until tomorrow!

PRINCIPAL WILSON. Oh, this isn't their show, this is their warm-up!

NEW DAWN.

AH!
THERE'S A LIGHT ON THE HORIZON
NOW THE NIGHT IS ALMOST GONE
SHINING BRIGHT, I KEEP MY EYES ON
A WORLD TO BUILD UPON
(Overlapping.) OH, I CAN SEE IN FRONT OF ME
OH, OH

(Clap, clap.)

A NEW DAWN

AH!

(*Variously.*) NOW WE CAN, NOW WE CAN
NOW WE CAN WAKE UP
NOW WE CAN, NOW WE CAN
TAKE UP OUR SONG
NOW WE CAN, NOW WE CAN
FINALLY SHAKE UP THE RULES
AND MAKE RIGHT OUR WRONGS

AH!
AH!
WHEN A NIGHTMARE PULLS YOU UNDER
AND YOU FIGHT THROUGH ALL THE LIES
YOU CAN WAKE UP NOW AND WONDER
AT WHAT LIGHTS THE SKIES
OH, I CAN SEE IN FRONT OF ME
OH, OH
A NEW DAWN
A NEW DAWN.
OH!

MELISSA SIMMS. (*To* **CAMERA OPERATOR**.) I LOVE them. Do you think they have merch?

RASMUSSON. "A New Dawn"! It's the perfect song! Did you write it for this weekend?

NEW DAWN. (*With attitude.*) No.

> (*The* **CHOIR** *turns, on the back of their jackets is emblazoned:* **NEW DAWN** *in rhinestones. They strike another pose and freeze.*)

> (*Music shifts.* **RASMUSSON** *continues to be interviewed as four* **HONOR STUDENTS** *enter, encumbered by bulky science equipment.*)

[MUSIC NO. 02A "LAB INTRO / UNDERSCORE"]

HONOR STUDENTS.
HOW I GOT HERE WAS NO ACCIDENT
I DESERVE TO TELL MY STORY
TIME NOW TO EXPERIMENT
LIFE IS JUST

ONE BIG
LAB'RATORY

RANDY. Whoa. This is it.

AURORA. Area 51.

REBECCA. That runway was long enough to land a space shuttle.

ELIOT. Guys, that's Melissa Simms, Channel 9 News!

REBECCA. Game face, Randy. Time to get that full-ride.

(*Turning.*) Principal Wilson?

(**WILSON** *doesn't hear.*)

Principal Wilson? Mom!

(**WILSON** *turns.*)

Where do we put all of our stuff?

PRINCIPAL WILSON. Hold on, Rebecca. Not sure yet.

RASMUSSON. (*Crossing to the students.*) And these are our young scientists I presume?

PRINCIPAL WILSON. Yes, the brightest and the best of Las Vegas Prep.

RASMUSSON. We've invited these four young scholars to spend the night here. They will have full security clearance and will perform a series of scientific experiments that pronounce Dreamland a safe, educational attraction for the whole family.

MELISSA. Their findings will be presented live tomorrow on Channel 9 News.

RASMUSSON. And one lucky student will be awarded full tuition to the college of their choosing, paid for by the US Government.

MELISSA. Now which of you is going to win? Tell us about yourselves.

REBECCA. Rebecca Wilson. Pilot. I've logged over 100 hours in the sky already. I'll be documenting all the aircraft I find on the base. Go Randy.

RANDY. I'm Randy. Geologist and Rebecca's boyfriend. I'll be scanning for radiation.

ELIOT. *(Into the camera.)* I'm Eliot Chambers. Meteorologist. I'll be studying atmospheric conditions. Back to you Melissa.

RASMUSSON. And you are?

AURORA. Oh. Aurora. I'll be looking at the stars. I mean, I'm into astronomy. I like space, and stars and...never mind.

RASMUSSON. The best and the brightest. It is my honor to welcome you to Dreamland, I look forward to your experiments –

[MUSIC NO. 02B "NEW DAWN ENDING"]

MELISSA. *(To* **CAMERA OPERATOR.***)* Ooooh! Keep rolling! I think the show choir is about to sing again!

NEW DAWN.

AH!
NOW WE CAN, NOW WE CAN
NOW WE CAN WAKE UP
NOW WE CAN, NOW WE CAN
TAKE UP OUR SONG
NOW WE CAN, NOW WE CAN
FINALLY SHAKE UP THE RULES
AND MAKE RIGHT OUR WRONGS

   (In a round.)

NOW WE CAN, NOW WE CAN
NOW WE CAN WAKE UP
NOW WE CAN, NOW WE CAN
TAKE UP OUR SONG
NOW WE CAN, NOW WE CAN
FINALLY SHAKE UP THE RULES
AND MAKE RIGHT OUR WRONGS
OH, OH

   (Hand claps.)

OH, OH

   (Hand claps.)

A NEW DAWN

A NEW DAWN
A NEW DAWN!
A NEW DAWN!

> *(From a corner,* **SNYDER** *applauds enthusiastically.)*

SNYDER. If music be the food of love, play on! Play on!

RASMUSSON. This is Snyder. He works at the facility. He'll be showing you where you will sleep and also where you can rehearse your material.

SNYDER. It will be my honor.

NEW DAWN SINGER #1. What do you do here? Scientist?

NEW DAWN SINGER #2. Pilot?

NEW DAWN SINGER #3. Armed guard?

SNYDER. Caretaker.

NEW DAWN SINGER #3. Huh?

NEW DAWN SINGER #2. He's the janitor.

NEW DAWN. *(Disappointed.)* Oh.

SNYDER. One should be raised to treat a janitor with the same respect as a CEO.

> *(He does a quick dance move.)*

Follow me.

> *(***SNYDER*** *exits.)*

QUINN. Did he just do a *(Insert whatever dance move he did: time-step, jeté, etc.)*?

RASMUSSON. *(Exiting.)* I have a good feeling about all of this.

> *(Segue directly to:)*

Scene Two

(On the other side of the hangar, **MELISSA SIMMS** *approaches* **PRINCIPAL WILSON** *and the* **HONOR STUDENTS**.*)*

MELISSA. Principal Wilson. I've got some good news and bad news.

PRINCIPAL WILSON. I'll take the –

MELISSA. Bad news: We're not going to have time in the segment tomorrow for each of your honor students to compete, so we'll have to pick one before we air.

PRINCIPAL WILSON. But Rasmusson said it was critical we get a scientific, aeronautic, astronomic, and geologic perspective.

MELISSA. Sure, that was until the network saw the show choir. Their perspective is learning more towards razzle dazzle. Whoever has the best experiment wins the scholarship and gets to present, got it?

REBECCA. But –

PRINCIPAL WILSON. You said there was good news?

MELISSA. Yes, well for some of them, definitely bad news for you. Colonel Rasmusson and I will be deciding who wins.

PRINCIPAL WILSON. But I was supposed to be one of the judges?

MELISSA. Sure, but that was until we learned the pilot is your daughter. How can you expect to be impartial?

PRINCIPAL WILSON. I treat my daughter like anyone else, right students?

REBECCA. Yes, Principal Wilson!

MELISSA. She was the only one who answered.

> *(Exiting.)*

You've got twenty-four hours. If you need me, I will be in my air-conditioned room in an undisclosed location.

REBECCA. Mom, you are ruining this for me!

PRINCIPAL WILSON. I'll talk to Rasmusson and see what I can do...

REBECCA. No! Don't do anything! You've done enough. Don't you see, the more time we're together the more it looks like you are trying to help me. Stay away. I will win this fair and square.

PRINCIPAL WILSON. Well, this is a good lesson for you, no special treatment. Here are the extra snacks and coconut water you asked for. You kids better get cracking! May the best scientist win!

(**PRINCIPAL WILSON** *exits.*)

REBECCA. We were all selected for our expertise, we all deserve to present. Now there's a lousy one in four chance.

ELIOT. You know when a forecaster says there is a twenty-five percent chance of rain it actually means it will rain on twenty-five percent of the days with exactly the same atmospheric conditions.

REBECCA. I don't know what to do with that, am I supposed to feel better or worse?

AURORA. I feel better. I didn't think I had a chance at all, but now, I'm strangely optimistic.

RANDY. If I win, you can have my place, Rebecca.

REBECCA. You shouldn't give up on this opportunity so quickly, baby bear. Although thank you, I'll hold you to it.

ELIOT. A fifty percent chance, there you go!

[MUSIC NO. 03 "LABORATORY LOOP"]

REBECCA. Coverage on national television means everything. And whoever wins can study anywhere they want!

AURORA. I guess I'd like to study astronomy at Cal Tech.

REBECCA. You can and you should.

ELIOT. Texas A & M has the best meteorology school in the country!

REBECCA. There you go Eliot! And for me, MIT then the Air Force Academy!

RANDY. I just want a school with a good chemistry program – close to MIT and the Air Force Academy!

HONOR STUDENTS. *(Variously.)*

> HOW I GOT HERE WAS NO ACCIDENT
> I DESERVE THE FAME AND GLORY
> TIME NOW TO EXPERIMENT
> LIFE IS JUST
> ONE BIG
> LAB'RATORY

[MUSIC NO. 04 "FOLLOW THE STARS"]

ELIOT. I'm going to set my weather balloon up over there, I need a lot of space.

REBECCA. I'm off to start documenting aircraft.

RANDY. I'm going to get some rock samples and start checking radiation levels.

REBECCA. Randy!

RANDY. Once I finish helping Rebecca.

AURORA. I'm going to set up my telescope and wait for it to get dark...by myself. Again. Always by myself...

> HERE ON THIS PLANET
> THE THIRD FROM THE SUN
> I DON'T REALLY FIT IN
> OR RELATE TO ANYONE
> BUT WHEN I LOOK UP
> AND THE STARS START TO SHINE
> I HAVE TO BELIEVE IN ALL OF THAT SKY
> THERE IS LIFE ON A PLANET
> THAT WILL BRING LIFE TO MINE
>
> LIFE IN A PREP SCHOOL
> IS BASIC'LLY HELL
> WHERE YOU SHRINK AND YOU DIE
> AND THEN GET SAVED BY THE BELL
> I KEEP MY HEAD DOWN
> IN ASTRONOMY TEXT

I READ AND I READ SO I AM PREPARED
SO I'M READY AND WAITING
FOR WHAT SCIENCE FINDS NEXT

THAT'S WHY I FOLLOW THE STARS
TO FIND WHAT MIGHT BE LIVING BEHIND THEIR
  SHINING LIGHT
THAT'S WHY I FOLLOW THE STARS
I PEEK INSIDE A TELESCOPE AND I'M A SATELLITE
WHEN I LOOK UP ALL I CAN SEE
IS ENDLESS POSSIBILITY
SO I FOLLOW, FOLLOW, FOLLOW THE STARS

I'LL FIND A PLANET
JUST LIGHT YEARS AWAY
WHERE I'M SURROUNDED BY FRIENDS
AND HAVE COOL THINGS TO SAY
I WON'T FEEL SO SCATTERED
AND LOST IN MY THOUGHTS
DOWN HERE ON EARTH I STAND WORLDS APART
BUT WHEN I'M STARGAZING
I'M CONNECTING THE DOTS

THAT'S WHY I FOLLOW THE STARS
TO SEARCH FOR WHAT IS OUT THERE
AND NOT FEEL SO ALONE
THAT'S WHY I FOLLOW THE STARS
IN ALL THOSE CONSTELLATIONS,
CAN I CALL ONE MY OWN?
I'LL LIVE THE LIFE I WISH I HAD
WITH NEIL DEGRASSE TYSON AS MY DAD
I FOLLOW, FOLLOW, FOLLOW, FOLLOW THE STARS!

THERE'S A HUNDRED THOUSAND MILLION
IN OUR GALAXY ALONE
THAT'S WHY I FOLLOW THE STARS
PLUS A MILLION OTHER GALAXIES
AND A MILLION STILL UNKNOWN
CHANCES ARE IN THAT GREAT ABYSS
THERE'S A PLANET THAT FITS ME BETTER THAN THIS
SO I FOLLOW, FOLLOW, FOLLOW, THE STARS!

(**AURORA** *stands up and starts to walk out of the hangar. She passes* **ELIOT**.*)*

ELIOT. Hey, where are you going?

AURORA. I'm bored. I'm gonna go find some aliens.

ELIOT. But there aren't any aliens.

AURORA. I've been listening to this podcast, it's stupid, but it's about these top-secret experiments that took place here. It talks about an underground bunker, where lots of highly classified stuff happened. I think I'm gonna go find it.

ELIOT. How? This facility is enormous.

AURORA. Well, I donated to the podcast and they sent me this map.

ELIOT. It's hand-drawn with an X.

AURORA. It was drawn from memory by an old scientist who used to work down there.

ELIOT. Sure it wasn't a pirate? This seems kind of off-limits. And a little crazy?

AURORA. The Colonel said we could go anywhere, and I think we should take him up on it. In the name of research and scientific discovery.

ELIOT. Cool, I'm in.

AURORA. Really?

ELIOT. Yeah. Help me get this weather balloon up and let's go!

AURORA. Okay. This is gonna be so awesome!

(**ELIOT** *motions to where he would like* **AURORA** *to move the balloon.)*

ELIOT. Thanks. I'm trying to stay presentable. If that reporter comes back in, I want to be camera-ready.

[MUSIC NO. 05 "WEATHERMAN"]

(*During the song,* **ELIOT** *tweaks the balloon's controls, showing its mechanics to* **AURORA**.*)*

AURORA. I love that you love weather.

ELIOT. Today high of seventy-five, low of forty-four, chance of precipitation zero percent.

AURORA. Wow. You're – that's remarkable.

ELIOT. It's not that hard. We live in the middle of a desert.

> ALL I'VE EVER WANTED
> IS TO BE THE SMILING GUY
> WITH THE VERY WHITE TEETH
> IN A VERY PLAYFUL TIE
> WHO LOOKS INTO THE CAMERA
> AND MOVES HIS HANDS LIKE SO
> AND ON THE SCREEN BEHIND HIM
> MAKES A COLD FRONT START TO BLOW
> I'LL SHARE THE FIVE-DAY FORECAST
> ALONG WITH SOLID CHRISTIAN VALUES
> ALL I'VE EVER WANTED
> IS TO BE ELIOT CHAMBERS, WEATHERMAN
> CHANNEL 9 NEWS
>
> ALL I'VE EVER WANTED
> IS TO BE THE KIND OF FELLA
> WHO DOLES OUT SAGE ADVICE
> LIKE, "YOU'LL BE NEEDING THAT UMBRELLA"
> I'LL GO OUT ON LOCATION
> IN A TRICKED OUT ACTION VAN
> AND SHARE SOME WEATHER WISECRACKS
> WITH MY PAL THE ANCHORMAN
> I WON'T GIVE THE HEADLINES
> OR BORING INTERVIEWS
> EV'RYONE WILL TUNE IN
> TO SEE ELIOT CHAMBERS WEATHERMAN
> CHANNEL 9 NEWS
>
> DOP. PLER.
> RAY. DAR.
> IS THERE ANYTHING MORE BEAUTIFUL THAN
> DOPPLER.
> RAYDAR.
> NO TWO WORDS MORE MUSICAL
>
> I FEEL IT IN MY WEATHER VEINS

THE HIGHS AND LOWS
THE FREEZING RAINS
I FEEL IT IN MY WEATHER VEINS
THE EPIC SNOWS, THE HURRICANES
I WILL CONTROL THE THUNDER
LIKE THE MIGHTY HANDS OF ZEUS!
ELIOT CHAMBERS WEATHERMAN
OF CHANNEL 9 NEWS –

> (**REBECCA** *and* **RANDY** *enter.* **RANDY** *transcribes everything* **REBECCA** *says.*)

REBECCA. So far two SR-71 Blackbirds, an A-12, three B-21s, a Red Box, very exciting, the first unmanned surveillance plane, and, I don't know what this is –

ELIOT. It's my weather balloon. I can move it if it's in your way –

REBECCA. No, it's fine.

ELIOT. Or, tell you about it?

REBECCA. If I'm going to document every aircraft on this base, I need to keep moving. Come along, Randy.

> (*She exits.*)

RANDY. Hey guys.

ELIOT. Everything okay?

RANDY. Oh sure, just running and walking on eggshells at the same time.

ELIOT. Are you and Rebecca fighting? Like a serious-possibly-it's-over-break-up kinda fight? I mean, I'm so sorry.

RANDY. She's pissed about having to compete, but don't worry, I'll help her collect great research, and then I can start working on my experiment.

ELIOT. Well let me know if I can help.

RANDY. It's okay, boyfriend duties.

REBECCA. (*Offstage.*) Randy! A Russian Mig!

RANDY. Coming! Is Mig spelled with one g or two?

> (**RANDY** *exits.*)

ELIOT. Rebecca is remarkable. You know she's a pilot right?

AURORA. I've heard.

ELIOT. I think she's the only person in our school that can fly a plane. Randy is one lucky dude.

ALL I'VE EVER WANTED
IS TO BE THE KIND OF GUY
WHO CARES ABOUT WHAT'S HAPP'NING
FOR PILOTS IN THE SKY
AND WHEN THERE IS BAD WEATHER
AND REBECCA'S STANDING BY
I'LL HAVE THE GUTS TO TALK TO HER
AND TELL HER WHERE TO FLY
AND WHEN SHE'S SAFELY LANDED
I PRAY SHE WON'T REFUSE
WHEN I ASK HER TO HAVE DINNER
WITH ELIOT CHAMBERS WEATHERMAN
CHANNEL 9 NEWS!

(They launch the weather balloon. As it rises:)

AURORA. So what does it do exactly?

ELIOT. Once the balloon hits a specific altitude it will start sending data to this app I built.

AURORA. You built an app?

ELIOT. Sure. See? You can monitor air pressure, wind speed, temperature, humidity, see, this facility claims to have been launching weather balloons for decades –

AURORA. What everyone thinks are UFOs.

ELIOT. Exactly. So, I'm gonna see if the readings they published, match the readings I get. If they do... Proof! No aliens. Now let's go find some aliens.

AURORA. I don't know if I'm holding this map correctly. This way?

*(***ELIOT*** flips the map around.)*

ELIOT. There.

AURORA. This way! You know Eliot, I'm glad we're doing this together.

ELIOT. Hey! We should invite Rebecca. I think she might find it really cool. And Randy of course.

AURORA. Do you think they'd even want to come?

ELIOT. I mean, what if we find a spaceship???! Of course they'd want to come!

AURORA. The more the merrier I guess.

ELIOT. Great, I'll go get them and be right back!

[MUSIC NO. 06 "FOLLOW THE STARS (REPRISE)"]

(**ELIOT** *runs off.*)

AURORA. Did I just make a friend? Or is he just using me? Don't screw this up. Let them think you're cool.

(**ELIOT** *returns with* **REBECCA** *and* **RANDY**.)

REBECCA. Heard you got a treasure map that leads to stupid aliens. Let's go.

AURORA.	ELIOT, RANDY & REBECCA.
	HOW I GOT HERE
THAT'S WHY I FOLLOW THE STARS	WAS NO ACCIDENT
TO SEARCH FOR WHAT IS OUT THERE	I DESERVE TO TELL MY STORY
AND NOT FEEL SO ALONE	TIME NOW TO EXPERIMENT
THAT'S WHY I FOLLOW THE STARS	LIFE IS JUST
IN ALL THOSE CONSTELLATIONS	ONE BIG
CAN I CALL ONE MY ONE?	LAB'RATORY
WHEN I LOOK UP ALL I CAN SEE	
IS ENDLESS POSSIBILITY	
SO I FOLLOW, FOLLOW, FOLLOW –	FOLLOW, FOLLOW, FOLLOW!
THE STARS!	

(*They follow the map out of the hangar.*)

[MUSIC NO. 06A "SCENE CHANGE"]

Scene Three

*(***NEW DAWN*** practices for the televised event.
RASMUSSON watches, as **SNYDER** mops in the
distance.)*

SCOTT. Alright gang, one more time from the top. Colonel
Rasmusson are you ready to pick your jaw up off the
floor?

RASMUSSON. Sure.

QUINN. Five, six, seven, eight!

[MUSIC NO. 07 "AREA 51"]

*(***NEW DAWN*** performs a glitzy Las Vegas style
number, complete with bedazzled lab coats
and an **ALIEN** in a rhinestone jumpsuit.)*

NEW DAWN BARITONES & BASSES.
DOO

NEW DAWN SOPRANOS, ALTOS & TENORS.
DOOT DOO DOO DOO...

NEW DAWN BARITONES & BASSES.
DOOT-DOO DOO

NEW DAWN SOPRANOS, ALTOS & TENORS.
DOOT DOO WAAH!

(Backing vocals continue throughout.)

NEW DAWN BARITONES & BASSES.	NEW DAWN SOPRANOS, ALTOS & TENORS.
JUST A HUNDRED MILES FROM VEGAS	DOOT DOO DOO DOO...
	DOOT DOO DOO DOO...
THERE IS SOMETHING	DOOT DOO DOO DOO...
SO OUTRAGEOUS	DOOT DOO DOOT DOO...
IT'S A SMALL BLACK OPS FACILITY	WAH DOO WAH
WITH LOTS OF CAPABILITY	DOO-WAH DOO-WAH
IT IS AREA	

NEW DAWN SOPRANOS, ALTOS & TENORS.
AREA WAH WAH

NEW DAWN BARITONES & BASSES.
>51!

NEW DAWN SOPRANOS, ALTOS & TENORS.
>AREA 51

NEW DAWN WOMEN.
>YEAH!

NEW DAWN TENORS.
>IT'S CALLED THE WORLD'S BEST
>WORST KEPT SECRET

NEW DAWN SOPRANOS, ALTOS & BASSES.	**NEW DAWN TENORS.**
DOO DOO DOO DOO	BUT CALL IT TONS OF FUN
BUT WE CALL IT TONS OF FUN	

NEW DAWN TENORS.
>IT IS

NEW DAWN.
>AREA, AREA, AREA
>AREA, AREA, AREA, AREA

NEW DAWN TENORS.
>51!

NEW DAWN SOPRANO, ALTO & BASSES.
>AREA 51!

NEW DAWN BARITONES & BASSES.	**NEW DAWN SOPRANOS, ALTOS & TENORS.**
SCIENTISTS	DOOT DOO DOOT DOO...
WERE SIPPING COFFEE	DOOT DOO DOOT DOO...
DROPPING BOMBS	DOOT DOO DOOT DOO
IN THE MOJAVE	DOOT DOO DOOT DOO
THEIR PROJECTS LACKED TRANSPARENCY	WAH DOO-WAH-DOO
WHICH LED TO SOME CONSPIRACY	WAH DOO-WAH
HERE AT	
AREA	AREA WAH WAH
51	

NEW DAWN SOPRANOS, ALTOS & TENORS.

AREA 51

NEW DAWN WOMEN.

YEAH!

NEW DAWN TENORS.	**NEW DAWN SOPRANOS, ALTOS & BASSES.**
IT'S CALLED THE WORLD'S BEST	DOOT DOO DOOT DOO
WORST KEPT SECRET	
	DOOT DOO
	JUST NOT SO SECRET
WE DON'T KNOW HOW IT WAS RUN	DOOT DOO DOOT DOO
	WE DON'T KNOW
	HOW IT WAS RUN

IT IS

NEW DAWN.

AREA, AREA, AREA,
AREA, AREA, AREA

NEW DAWN TENORS.

51!

NEW DAWN SOPRANOS, ALTOS & BASSES.

AREA 51!

NEW DAWN.

TAKE THE E.T. HIGHWAY
KEEP YOUR EYES UP TO THE SKY
MAYBE YOU'LL SEE ONE OF THE BASE'S FAMOUS FLYING
    UFOS
THEY'VE GOT SPY PLANES, BOMBERS, WHIRLIGIGS
STEALTH PLANES, DRONES, AND RUSSIAN MIGS
AND THAT'S JUST WHAT THEY'RE WILLING TO DISCLOSE!

*(**SCOTT** appears wearing the alien head and
jumpsuit.)*

NEW DAWN BARITONES & BASSES.

NOTHING ELSE TO DISCLOSE!

NEW DAWN ALTOS, TENORS & BASSES.

NEW DAWN SOPRANOS.

SO HEAD OVER	SO HEAD O... SO HEAD
SO HEAD ON OVER TO NEVADA HEAD TO NEVADA	OVER TO NEVADA
WHAT YOU HAVE HEARD	WHAT YOU'VE HEARD
IT DOESN'T IT DOESN'T MATT-AH	IT DOESN'T MATT-AH!

NEW DAWN.

THEY PUT THE EXTRA IN TERRESTRIAL

(Short sensible tap break.)

NO LONGER ADVERSARIAL

(Another short sensible tap break.)

NEW DAWN TENORS.

IT IS

NEW DAWN.

AREA, AREA,
AREA, AREA
AREA, AREA,
AREA, AREA
AREA, AREA,
AREA 51!

SO COME ON OUT TO AREA 51
YEAH!

> *(General* **NEW DAWN** *hubbub of how well that went, and how they are sure their performance will slay on television.* **RASMUSSON** *approaches them.)*

RASMUSSON. It's remarkable. You really are triple threats. Triple threats to the security of this base! There's a few things we'll need to tweak for your performance. May I see the music?

QUINN. *(Handing over the music.)* Hi Colonel Rasmusson, I'm Quinn, the student-elected choreographer.

RASMUSSON. Did you write this?

SCOTT. No, I did. I'm Scott.

RASMUSSON. Right. The mask maker.

SCOTT. Among other things.

RASMUSSON. Give me a moment.

> *(The students watch in horror as* **RASMUSSON** *pulls out a sharpie and starts to black out lyrics in the song. There are audible gasps as it happens.)*

I'll have a talk with your principal, but I thought I made it very clear the musical celebration is to be about the history of Dreamland, not the conspiracies surrounding it. Here. Your song is now approved by the US Government. Happy rehearsing. Oh, and cut the alien head.

> *(***RASMUSSON*** *exits. The kids huddle around the marked-up music.)*

SCOTT. Sweet Lin-Manuel Miranda, I have been officially censored.

NEW DAWN SINGER #2. What do we do with all the lyrics he crossed out?

QUINN. Rewrite them.

SCOTT. Are you kidding? There's more blacked out here than the Mueller report! I'm not going through this again.

QUINN. Let's try the song, but this time don't sing the marked-out words.

[MUSIC NO. 08 "AREA 51 (REDACTED"]

> *(Performance note:* **NEW DAWN** *hums "HmmHmm" over all redacted text.)*

NEW DAWN BARITONES & BASSES.
DOO

NEW DAWN SOPRANOS, ALTOS & TENORS.

    DOOT DO DOO DOO...

NEW DAWN BARITONES & BASSES.

    DOOT-DOO DOO

NEW DAWN SOPRANOS, ALTOS & TENORS.

    DOOT DOO WAAH!

      (Background vocals continue.)

NEW DAWN BASSES.

    JUST A HUNDRED MILES FROM VEGAS
    THERE IS SOMETHING SO OUTRAGEOUS
    IT'S A SMALL BLACK OPS FACILITY
    WITH LOTS OF CAPABILITY
    IT IS ██████

NEW DAWN SOPRANOS, ALTOS & TENORS.

    ██████ ██████ ██████

NEW DAWN BARITONES & BASSES.

    ██████ ██████ ██████

NEW DAWN SOPRANOS, ALTOS & TENORS.

    ██████ ██████ ██████
    ██████ ██████ ██████

    YEAH!

NEW DAWN BARITONES & BASSES.	**NEW DAWN SOPRANOS, ALTOS & TENORS.**
IT'S CALLED THE WORLD'S BEST	DOOT DOO DOOT DOO
WORST KEPT SECRET	DOOT DO JUST NOT SO SECRET
BUT WE CALL IT TONS OF FUN	DOOT DOO DOOT DOO
	WE CALL IT TONS OF FUN
IT IS	

NEW DAWN.

    ██████ , ██████ , ██████
    ██████ , ██████ , ██████
    ██████ , ██████ , ██████
    ██████ , ██████ , ██████

NEW DAWN BARITONES & BASSES.

!

NEW DAWN SOPRANOS, ALTOS & TENORS.

NEW DAWN.

TAKE THE E.T. HIGHWAY
KEEP YOUR EYES UP TO THE SKY,
MAYBE YOU'LL SEE ONE OF THE BASE'S FAMOUS FLYING
████!
THEY'VE GOT ████ ████, ████ ████, WHIRLIGIGS,
████ ████, DRONES, AND ████ ████
AND THAT'S JUST WHAT THEY'RE WILLING TO ████████!
IT IS
████, ████, ████
████, ████, ████
████, ████, ████
████, ████, ████
████, ████, ████
████, ████, ████
████, ████, ████
████, ████, ████!
SO COME ON OUT TO ████ ██
YEAH!

> *(The song ends, it is very quiet, a malaise sets
> in.)*

SCOTT. We are not doing this song.

NEW DAWN SINGER #1. Yeah, it feels like something's
missing.

SCOTT. Yeah! Half of my lyrics.

QUINN. We'll tweak the choreography, it'll be fine.

SCOTT. I'm never getting into NYU!

NEW DAWN SINGER #2. Why does he want to cut so much of the song? I mean, none of the things we were singing about were actual secrets.

QUINN. Scott will write something new.

SCOTT. Oh sure...

QUINN. There's a hole in our show, we just have to fill the hole...

SCOTT. It's not a Mad Lib! You have no respect for the artistic process. None of you!!!

> *(From a dark corner of the hangar.)*

SNYDER. I do.

> *(**NEW DAWN** turns and finally sees the strange man lurking in the corner.)*

NEW DAWN. *(Screaming.)* AHHHHHH!

SNYDER. *(Quoting the lyric.)*
THE PROJECTS LACKED TRANSPARENCY
WHICH LED TO SOME CONSPIRACY.
That's good.

NEW DAWN. Who are you?

SNYDER. I've been here the whole time. Snyder.

NEW DAWN SINGER #3. Stranger danger.

SNYDER. I took you to this hangar? I'm your government appointed chaperone? The caretaker?

QUINN. Oh. He's the janitor.

NEW DAWN. *(Disappointed.)* Oh.

SNYDER. Believe me, it was not my dream job. You see, I come from a long line of caretakers, and I swore to thirteen-year-old me, Snyder, you are not going to follow in the footsteps of your grandfather, grandmother, mother, and father. All of 'em worked here. My grandparents died of radiation poisoning. Which is why when I was about your age I went to Vegas to become a star.

NEW DAWN SINGER #1. *(On top of each other.)* Really? We're from Vegas!

NEW DAWN SINGER #2. My dad works for Cirque du Soleil.

SCOTT. What's your vocal range?

NEW DAWN SINGER #3. Have we seen you in anything?

SNYDER. No. I got a job scrubbing toilets at Circus Circus.

NEW DAWN SINGER #1. Well, at least it's a circus.

QUINN. It's a casino.

NEW DAWN SINGER #2. Yeah, a crappy casino.

SNYDER. But I never gave up on my dream. Until I did. Once my parents died from radiation poisoning, I had to come back... Someone needed to clean this place. So I picked up my mother's toolbox and my father's plunger and got to work. It's a pretty lonely gig. Never allowed in bunkers where anything interesting was happening, never allowed to talk to the pilots, or scientists, just clean up after them. But sometimes when I'm all alone, I close my eyes and imagine all those people out there in the dark.

[MUSIC NO. 09 "SHOW ME THE STAGE"]

SCOTT. *(Whispering to* **QUINN**.*)* What's happening?

QUINN. Not sure, just go with it.

> (**SNYDER** *sings, it's gentle and haunting, and kind of great.)*

SNYDER.
 IT COULD BE ON BROADWAY
 IT COULD BE THE MET
 PUT ME IN A LOUNGE ACT
 OR BARBERSHOP QUARTET
 IT COULD BE A BOY BAND
 WITH SINGERS HALF MY AGE
 I JUST WANT THAT HOT LIGHT
 SO TURN ON THE SPOTLIGHT
 SHOW ME THE STAGE!

 IT COULD BE A CRUISE SHIP
 OR A KARAOKE ROOM
 I'LL SING CHRISTMAS CAROLS

DOOR TO DOOR IN JUNE
PUT ME IN A DOT GIF OR DOT JIF
I KNOW THEY'RE ALL THE RAGE
I JUST WANT EXPOSURE
NOT THAT TYPE OF EXPOSURE
SHOW ME THE STAGE!

IT COULD BE EQUITY
NON-EQUITY, COMMUNITY THEATRE
A TALENT SHOW, A FREAK SHOW
OR SOMETHING WEIRDER
IT COULD BE A COUNTY FAIR OR A LAS VEGAS BUFFET
I'LL SING THE STAR-SPANGLED BANNER AT A YMCA
A CAMPFIRE, A HIGH WIRE
A TOWN CRIER, A SHOW CHOIR!

> (**NEW DAWN** *gets into it, becoming his back-up choir.*)

SNYDER.	NEW DAWN.
IT COULD BE A BIG HIT	AAH…
IT COULD BE A FLOP	
LET ME LET MY VOICE RING OUT	AAH…
'STEAD OF THIS MOP	
ALL I AM IS A BIRD	AAH!
IN AN UNDERGROUND CAGE	
I'LL BE SERENADING, NOT DECONTAMINATING	AAH… AAH…
SHOW ME THE STAGE	AAH…
SHOW ME –	

QUINN. *(To* **SCOTT**.*)* Are you thinking what I'm thinking?

SCOTT. …fill the hole…

QUINN. Would you like to…join the New Dawn show choir?

SNYDER. *(Shaking hands.)* I thought you'd never ask.

SNYDER.	NEW DAWN.
THE STAGE!	AAH! AAH! AAH!

[MUSIC NO. 9A "SCENE CHANGE"]

Scene Four

(A subterranean laboratory in the bowels of "Area 51." On stage is a giant spaceship, being worked on by a group of **ALIENS**. *These* **ALIENS** *are more human than one would think, but with a few odd attributes.)*

[MUSIC NO. 10 "UNTIL THE DAY"]

ALIENS.
UNTIL THE DAY
THEY OPEN THAT DOOR
UNTIL THE DAY
THEY OPEN THAT DOOR
KEEP CALM, CARRY ON
IS WHAT THEY LIKE TO SAY
UNTIL THE DAY
THEY OPEN THAT DOOR

ALIEN MEN.
OH OH
OH OH

OBERON.
WE ONCE WERE EXPLORERS OF THE GALAXIES
THE COSMOS WE COMBED FOR CURIOSITIES

TITANIA.
WE FOLLOWED SOME MUSIC TO THE MILKY WAY

OBERON & TITANIA.
AND FOR SIXTY YEARS IT'S WHERE WE'VE HAD TO STAY

TITANIA.
LOCKED INSIDE A SILVER CELL
FOR SIXTY YEARS

OBERON.
NO ONE KNOWS THAT WE'RE ALIVE

OBERON & TITANIA.
OR TRAPPED DOWN HERE
WE USED TO BRAVELY GO
WHERE NONE HAD GONE BEFORE
NOW WE WAIT AND WAIT

UNTIL THEY OPEN THAT DOOR

ALIENS.
UNTIL THE DAY
THEY OPEN THAT DOOR
UNTIL THE DAY
THEY OPEN THAT DOOR
KEEP CALM, CARRY ON
IS WHAT THEY LIKE TO SAY
UNTIL THE DAY
THEY OPEN THAT DOOR

ALIEN MEN.
OH

PUCK.
OH WHEN WE CRASH LANDED ALL THOSE YEARS AGO
WE CRAWLED FROM THE WRECKAGE AND WE SAID
HELLO

PUCK, PEASEBLOSSOM, COBWEB, MOTH & MUSTARDSEED.
THERE WAS NO PARTY OR BACCHANAL
OH THE HUMANS STOOD AND SAID NOTHING AT ALL

OBERON, TITANIA, PUCK, PEASEBLOSSOM, COBWEB, MOTH & MUSTARDSEED.
SOMEHOW WHEN THEY LOOK AT US
WE DISAPPEAR
WE'RE A SIGHT THEY CAN'T SEE
A SOUND THEY CAN'T HEAR
THEY TOOK OUR SHIP
WE FOLLOWED IT
DOWN TO THIS FLOOR
NOW WE WAIT AND WAIT
UNTIL THEY OPEN THAT DOOR!

ALIENS.
UNTIL THE DAY
THEY OPEN THAT DOOR
UNTIL THE DAY
THEY OPEN THAT DOOR
KEEP CALM, CARRY ON
IS WHAT THEY LIKE TO SAY
UNTIL THE DAY

THEY OPEN THAT DOOR

IF ONLY THEY COULD HEAR US
IF ONLY THEY COULD SEE
WE CAME BECAUSE WE FOLLOWED A RADIO FREQUENCY
WE CAN SPEAK THEIR LINGO:
"DADDY-O, LET'S ROCK AND ROLL!"
WE CAN DO THE LATEST DANCES
THE TWIST AND THE STROLL

PUCK.
IF ONLY THEY KNEW WE WERE ALIVE

PUCK, COBWEB, PEASEBLOSSOM, MOTH & MUSTARDSEED.
WE COULD MAKE CONTACT
AND REALLY CONNECT
OVER THE RADIO HITS OF 1955

PUCK. The first day I'm free I am hopping in a Ford Fairlane and going to a drive-in movie!

OBERON. No Puck. When that door opens we are getting off this planet as quickly as possible.

MUSTARDSEED & MOTH. But don't you want to go to a sock hop?

PEASEBLOSSOM & COBWEB. Watch more *American Bandstand*?

PUCK. It's why we're here!

OBERON. This mission was a fool's errand. We must continue to practice disassembling and reassembling the ship, so that when that door opens we are ready.

ALIENS.
UNTIL THE DAY
THEY OPEN THAT DOOR
UNTIL THE DAY
THEY OPEN THAT DOOR
WE'LL FIX OUR SHIP
AND WAIT FOR MORE
UNTIL THE DAY
THEY OPEN THAT DOOR
THEY OPEN THAT DOOR
THEY OPEN THAT DOOR

THEY OPEN THAT DOOR

(The door opens. A hazy shaft of light fills the space.)

PUCK. Look everyone!! The door!

AURORA. *(Creeping in.)* Hello? Is there anybody in here?

*(The **ALIENS** erupt in cheers and applause. Note: The humans cannot see or hear the **ALIENS**.)*

RANDY. Hello?

*(The **ALIENS** cheer and applaud again. The humans do not acknowledge.)*

AURORA. It's empty.

*(The **ALIENS** surround the **FOUR** and listen.)*

ELIOT. Do you think this is the room on the map?

AURORA. It must be.

(The door slowly closes...)

REBECCA. Wait, there's no handle on the inside. Randy! Don't close the door!

PUCK. The door is closing everyone!

HONOR STUDENTS & ALIENS. Ahhhhh!

RANDY. *(Running over to the door.)* Got it! Just in time.

(Catches it and puts a nearby broom in the door to keep it from fully shutting.)

ELIOT. We're so far down, do you think we're past the crust of the earth and near the mantle?

RANDY. No way dude, our skulls would implode if we were THAT deep. *(Looks at his Geiger counter.)* FYI, I'm registering very little radioactivity.

TITANIA. What has happened to these humans? Where are the poodle skirts and cardigan sweaters? Shouldn't they all be smoking cigarettes?

AURORA. I can't believe we found it! It's like an enormous hangar for planes but underground.

REBECCA. I mean, obviously. What did you think it was gonna be? I mean, look at that huge Russian spy plane over there.

AURORA. I don't think that's a Russian spy plane, Rebecca.

REBECCA. Come on, it totally is. It HAS to be. Look at the engines. Totally out of the Sikorsky era, like World War I, this is incredible!

AURORA. I think it's an alien ship.

(**ALIENS** *applaud and cheer.*)

PUCK. The girl shall save us!

COBWEB & PEASEBLOSSOM. Save us girl!

MOTH & MUSTARDSEED. Save us!

OBERON. Quiet! They continue…

REBECCA. Whatever this is, it's a rare find.

RANDY. How rare?

REBECCA. Like, I've never seen a picture of it anywhere, and I've seen everything.

AURORA. The craftsmanship is stunning.

RANDY. But why is it all the way down here?

AURORA. Aliens.

(*The* **ALIENS** *applaud again.*)

REBECCA. Ridiculous. I know you're into space and stars and all but come on. Also, we're supposed to NOT find aliens remember?

OBERON. We need to disassemble our ship now while the door is still open.

TITANIA. And yet how do we do that without creating a panic?

PUCK. I can do it! Listen to me! I've invented something that can help!

TITANIA. If the humans see us moving parts of the ship it will only create more chaos.

PUCK. Yeah, to them it will look like this:

*(**PUCK** picks up object and "floats" it in front of **AURORA**.)*

AURORA. Did you see that?

REBECCA. What?

AURORA. Never mind.

TITANIA. Exactly. And that will probably lead to us being trapped for another sixty years.

OBERON. We will need to distract the humans.

REBECCA. I wanna get some measurements of this thing. And some pics.

RANDY. Yeah. Hey, come here.

(Takes his phone out to take a picture.)

REBECCA. Naturally.

TITANIA. Ooh! Is that the new pocket transistor radio? *(Beat.)* It's very quiet.

*(They take a quick selfie and then take one with just **REBECCA** in front of the engine.)*

*(Maybe **RANDY** takes his own, maybe the **ALIENS** photobomb them. **REBECCA** continues taking measurements and photos.)*

AURORA. It's uncanny how everything the podcast said is turning out to be true.

REBECCA. That might be a little bit of a stretch Aurora.

RANDY. Clearly there are no aliens here, if there were, I think we'd have seen them by now.

AURORA. Other life forms exist, I know it. I can feel it. I feel like they're all around us.

*(The **ALIENS** cheer and applaud.)*

PUCK. I like this one.

COBWEB, PEASEBLOSSOM, MUSTARDSEED & MOTH. I do too.

TITANIA. I'll like her more if she can get us out of here.

OBERON. No, we must not rely on the humans.

REBECCA. I don't think you're gonna meet any aliens down here.

RANDY. Unless you count Eliot.

ELIOT. Guys, I'm definitely from Las Vegas.

AURORA. Whatever, take my picture, Eliot.

ELIOT. OK.

        (**ALIENS** *photobomb the shot.*)

REBECCA. OK, ten more minutes, then back to the experiments!

OBERON. We must be smart about this. When the humans leave, I think you six should follow them. Find the perfect spot to reassemble and launch our ship and create a diversion so we can move the pieces to it without the humans noticing.

PUCK. Or you can let me try to communicate with my invention.

OBERON. No. We tried everything, and all they did was lock us down here.

AURORA. Poor creatures. They must not have survived.

PUCK. Oh, we survived! We live for hundreds of your Earth years!

AURORA. I wonder if they were locked in cages. Actually I bet cages were inadequate because their bodies were more like energy than a coagulation of mass.

PUCK. Actually, we're more like light!

REBECCA. I don't know how that's possible, but you do you.

RANDY. Good luck getting a full ride with that kind of hypothesis, dummy.

ELIOT. Yeah, the map was one thing; now you're just grabbing at straws.

AURORA. You guys are gonna rue the day you made fun of me.

OBERON. I've seen enough. Help these young Earthlings towards the door so we can plan our hasty exit.

COBWEB, PEASEBLOSSOM, MOTH & MUSTARDSEED. *(Mischievous glint in their eyes.)* We thought you'd never ask!

> *(They knock something over.)*

RANDY. Ummmm guys, did you just see that?

ELIOT. I did.

AURORA. Me too.

REBECCA. What?

ELIOT. That… There. Just fell over…by itself.

AURORA. Aliens!!

> *(**ALIENS** applaud.)*

RANDY. I'm definitely not scared right now, but maybe let's go.

REBECCA. Come on!

> *(Makes a break for it, and is the first one out.)*

RANDY. *(Following.)* We're outta here!

> *(They exit. **AURORA** is last, she turns back.)*

AURORA. Bye aliens! I just want you to know… I believe!

> *(She swings the door wide which gives enough time for:)*

OBERON. Go, go, go! Be swift! Make haste!

> *(**PUCK**, **TITANIA**, **MUSTARDSEED**, **MOTH**, **COBWEB**, and **PEASEBLOSSOM** exit along with the **HONOR STUDENTS**. The door shuts.)*

Our journey home is nigh. Let's get to work!!

[MUSIC NO. 11 "UNTIL THE DAY (REPRISE)"]

ALIENS.
> UNTIL THE DAY
> THEY REOPEN THAT DOOR
> UNTIL THE DAY
> THEY REOPEN THAT DOOR
> KEEP CALM, CARRY ON

IS WHAT THEY LIKE TO SAY
UNTIL THE DAY
THEY REOPEN THAT DOOR
THEY REOPEN THAT DOOR
THEY REOPEN THAT DOOR
THEY REOPEN THAT DOOR

Scene Five

(The **HONOR STUDENTS** *make their way through endless corridors, followed by* **TITANIA, PUCK, MUSTARDSEED, MOTH, COBWEB,** *and* **PEASEBLOSSOM.***)*

RANDY. How do we get back above ground, Aurora?

AURORA. Give me a minute. The map wasn't completely accurate, I made a few educated guesses before we stumbled into that lab.

REBECCA. Don't tell me we're lost.

AURORA. Not lost. Exploring. And I'm not ready to go back just yet. There is something down here. I can feel it.

REBECCA. This is the stairway we came down right?

AURORA. I think so?

RANDY. You'd think there'd be more exit signs.

ELIOT. It's a secret underground facility.

AURORA. Meaning, whatever they're hiding down here, they want it forgotten.

REBECCA. Or, no one's been down here for decades, so nothing's up to code? What does it matter, we're still lost. Why did you even invite us Eliot?

ELIOT. Don't look at me, this was Aurora's stupid idea!

AURORA. Well I'm sorry!

REBECCA. You should be!

RANDY. I'm hungry!

REBECCA. Me too!

ELIOT. *(Diffusing.)* Just in case we missed a staircase, we should double-check these two hallways. I'll take this one.

AURORA. I'll go that way.

REBECCA. I'm going to sit right here on these steps and chew some gum, pretend it's a sandwich, and finish up my report. I'll give you ten minutes, and then I'm heading up. Randy stay with me.

RANDY. Can I have some sandwich gum?

REBECCA. Of course, baby bear.

> *(The* **STUDENTS** *split up.)*

TITANIA. *(To* **PUCK**, **MOTH**, **MUSTARDSEED**.*)* You three stay on this level with the humans. We will go above ground and find a suitable launchpad.

PUCK. With your permission, I'd like to try and communicate with them one last time.

TITANIA. Puck –

PUCK. If we don't make contact this whole trip has been for nothing!

TITANIA. This trip will be for nothing if we never make it home.

PUCK. But we're so close.

TITANIA. These humans are self-involved and incompetent! Except for the sad girl that no one listens to.

PUCK. I think my invention will work!

TITANIA. Puck, your commander is giving you a direct order.

PUCK. Co-commander.

TITANIA. And you are a neophyte on your first mission!

PUCK. It's been over sixty years!

TITANIA. Stay with the humans. Gather intel and observe from afar. We will rendezvous above ground. And Puck, no trouble!

> *(She leaves with* **PEASEBLOSSOM** *and* **COBWEB**. **PUCK** *stews.)*

[MUSIC NO. 12 "TWO STEPS AHEAD"]

PUCK.
> FOLLOW THE RULES, PUCK
> OBEY THE COMMAND
> YOU KNOW WHO RULES, PUCK
> THE PLAN HAS BEEN PLANNED
> AND THOUGH I AM THE YOUNGEST,
> I DON'T LEAD, I GET LED

I'M THE ONLY ONE WHO SEES
TWO STEPS AHEAD

WHILE EV'RYONE WAS FIXING
BUILDING, AND REPAIRING
I WAS IN THE CORNER
QUIETLY PREPARING
THEY ALL FORGOT THE DREAM
OF WHAT WE CAME TO DO
BUT I STILL HAVE A SCHEME
A WAY OF BREAKING THROUGH
SURE, OUR SURVIVAL MIGHT HANG BY A THREAD
BUT I'M THE ONLY ONE WHO'S THINKING TWO STEPS
    AHEAD

> (**PUCK** *removes a pair of glasses that resemble*
> *original 3-D glasses with red and blue lenses*
> *and shows them to* **MOTH** *and* **MUSTARDSEED.**)

I QUIETLY INVENTED
WITH NO SUPERVISION
SOMETHING THAT ENHANCES
HUMAN FIELD OF VISION
YOU HOOK THEM, ROUND THE EAR
AND SUDDENLY THEY SEE,
OUR BODIES WILL APPEAR
AND IT'S ALL THANKS TO ME
ONCE AGAIN I'M THINKING TWO STEPS AHEAD

MOTH & MUSTARDSEED.
    SEE HOW ONE SIDE OF IT'S BLUE AND THE OTHER IS RED!
PUCK.
    THE LENSES ARE UNIQUE
    A PAIN TO CALIBRATE
PUCK, MOTH & MUSTARDSEED.
    MADE SO ONE CAN SEE
    THE UV LIGHT WE RADIATE
PUCK.
    THEY'RE JUST A PROTOTYPE
    BUT MIGHT GO OVER BIG

PUCK, MOTH & MUSTARDSEED.

ALL WE NEED'S A HUMAN SUBJECT
AS OUR GUINEA PIG!

MOTH & MUSTARDSEED.

BUT THERE'S OUR CO-COMMANDER
WE SHOULD NOT DISCOUNT HER

PUCK.

SHE THINKS THEY'RE UNWORTHY
OF A CLOSE ENCOUNTER

MOTH & MUSTARDSEED.

REMEMBER WHAT SHE SAID
SHE CALLED THEM TEENAGE FOOLS

PUCK.

INSIDE THIS METAL SHED
THEY'RE NOT THE SHARPEST TOOLS

PUCK, MOTH & MUSTARDSEED.

IF THIS GOES WRONG WE COULD ALL END UP DEAD
IS THIS THE RIGHT TIME TO BE THINKING TWO STEPS
    AHEAD?

MOTH & MUSTARDSEED.

BUT ONE OF THEM'S COOL, PUCK

PUCK.

ONE OF THEM'S NICE

MOTH & MUSTARDSEED.

THE OTHER THREE SUCK, PUCK
THEY NEED YOUR DEVICE

PUCK.

I'LL HAVE SOME FUN AND MAYBE
SAVE THE DAY AS WELL

PUCK, MOTH & MUSTARDSEED.

YOU'RE THE ONLY ONE WHO SEES
TWO STEPS AHEAD

SO GO ON, CAST YOUR SPELL!

> (**ELIOT** *turns a corner and comes face to face
> with* **PUCK**, *although he doesn't see her.*)

ELIOT. *(To himself.)* I know this hallway. I've been in this
  hallway. This is not good.

> (**PUCK** *takes out her glasses, and
> ceremoniously slips them onto* **ELIOT**'s *face.*)

PUCK. Simple man, upon your eyes I throw
  All the power this charm doth owe.
  Though you can't hear me, these shall be
  New eyes for a new world to see!

> (**ELIOT** *blinks his eyes. The music swells,
> and the world is now in glorious 1950s
> Technicolor a la "Mr. Sandman." With every
> "BUM" a shock of energy shoots through a
> different part of* **ELIOT**'s *body.*)

[MUSIC NO. 13 "AURORA"]

MOTH & MUSTARDSEED WITH OFFSTAGE ANGELIC VOICES.
  BUM BUM BUM BUM
  BUM BUM BUM BUM
  BUM BUM BUM BUM BUM!

ELIOT.
  I CAN'T BELIEVE IT

PUCK. It's working!

ELIOT.
  HAVE YOU COME FROM ABOVE?

PUCK. Yes! Yes I have.

ELIOT.
  YOU MUST BE AN ANGEL

PUCK. Nooooo.

ELIOT.
  THIS MUST BE LOVE!

PUCK. Wait a second –

> (**ELIOT** *walks right past* **PUCK** *and kneels
> before* **AURORA**.)

ELIOT.
  YOU MAKE THE WORLD GLOW

WITH YOUR POWERFUL AURA
MY LADY, MEINE DAMEN
MY BELLA, SEÑORA
AURORA! AURORA!
AURORA! AURORA!

AURORA. Are you talking to me?

*(**PUCK** takes the glasses off* **ELIOT**.*)*

PUCK. Well, that didn't work. Does he still have feelings for her without the glasses?

ELIOT. Can I get you anything? Are you hungry? Thirsty? Can you I wash your feet? Do you need a kiss?

AURORA. What?

PUCK. Oh no. Never to worry. A few tweaks.

*(**PUCK** adjusts the lenses.)*

AURORA. Eliot, are you feeling alright?

ELIOT. Oh, I'm *feeling* alright. Here, take my blazer.

AURORA. Thanks. It is a little cold in here.

*(She puts on his blazer. **RANDY** enters.)*

RANDY. Hey guys, Rebecca says it's been ten minutes. You ready to head up?

PUCK. That should do it. Let's try a fresh test subject.

*(**PUCK** puts the glasses on **RANDY**. And stands back. The same romantic musical sweep, as shocks shoot through **RANDY**'s body with every "BUM.")*

MOTH & MUSTARDSEED WITH OFFSTAGE ANGELIC VOICES.
BUM BUM BUM BUM
BUM BUM BUM BUM
BUM BUM BUM BUM BUM!

RANDY.
I CAN'T BELIEVE IT!

PUCK. So far so good.

RANDY.
YOU ARE OUT OF THIS WORLD!

PUCK. I am! Yes! I am!

RANDY.

　WILL YOU BE MY LOVER?

PUCK. Not again.

RANDY.

　MY ARMS ARE UNFURLED

　　　(**RANDY** *runs to* **AURORA**.)

　YOU MAKE THE WORLD GLOW

　WITH YOUR POWERFUL AURA

　YOU'RE SWEET AS A PIE

　AND AS SOFT AS... ANGORA!

　AURORA! AURORA!

　AURORA! AURORA!

AURORA. What are you doing? Get away from me!

　　　(**PUCK** *plucks the glasses off of* **RANDY** *and*
　　　watches dumbfounded as the **GUYS** *vie for*
　　　AURORA's *attention*.)

RANDY & ELIOT WITH MUSTARDSEED, MOTH & ANGELIC VOICES.

　BUM BUM BUM BUM

　BUM BUM BUM BUM

　BUM BUM BUM BUM BUM!

ELIOT.

　YOUR NAME IS A RAINBOW

　FOLLOWING A STORM

RANDY.

　A NUCLEAR REACTOR

　PERPETUALLY WARM

RANDY & ELIOT.

　YOU'RE THE CUTEST WOODLAND FAUNA

　THE BRIGHTEST ISLAND FLORA

　I WANNA TELL THE WORLD

　ABOUT THE ONE THAT I ADORE

　AURORA! AURORA!

　(At the same time.) You like her too?

　AURORA! AURORA!

　AURORA! AURORA!

AURORA! AURORA!
AURORA!

(By the end of the song, **REBECCA** *has entered, she sees the* **GUYS** *draped over* **AURORA**.*)*

REBECCA. Randy. Why are you holding Aurora's hand while at the same time giving her a back massage?

RANDY. My dear Aurora has had an incredibly stressful day. She needs to relax.

ELIOT. If you are tired, let me crouch and be a sturdy footstool for you, or if you'd like to go, I am more than happy to offer you a piggyback ride up the stairs.

AURORA. I need both of you to stop. This is not funny. I know what you all think of me, but you don't have to mock me to my face. Just – leave me alone!

(She runs off.)

RANDY & ELIOT. Aurora!

RANDY. My darling –

ELIOT. My sweet –

RANDY & ELIOT. Come back!

(They follow her.)

REBECCA. My *darling*? RANDY!

(She chases after them. **PUCK** *is still fiddling with the glasses.)*

PUCK. Perhaps if I adjust the... Foolish humans, wait for me!

*(**PUCK** exits followed by* **MOTH** *and* **MUSTARDSEED***.)*

Scene Six

[MUSIC NO. 14 "23,360"]

(In a dark corner of the **ALIENS***' cell, an* **ALIEN** *approaches* **OBERON** *who is scratching something into a wall.)*

ALIEN #1. Oberon, the ship is disassembled and ready to be transported.

OBERON. Good. Now we wait.

ALIEN #1. Any word from those on the other side of the door?

OBERON. Not yet, but do not fear. They will return with a solution.

ALIEN #1. And we will go home?

OBERON. Yes. Sleep now. Tomorrow we go home.

(The **ALIENS** *sleep in a cool-alien way.* **OBERON** *goes back to scratching on the wall, light reveals it is a tally of the days they have been trapped underground. The scratches cover most of the room.)*

TWENTY-THREE THOUSAND THREE HUNDRED AND SIXTY
THE TOTAL INCLUDING THIS MARK
NOW AS THE NIGHT COMES I PRAY THAT THIS DAY IS
THE LAST WE ARE KEPT IN THE DARK

I ALWAYS FEARED I WOULD DO THIS FOREVER
OR RUN OUT OF ROOM ON THE WALL
TWENTY-THREE THOUSAND THREE HUNDRED AND SIXTY
I MIGHT LEAVE SOME SPACE AFTER ALL

(On the other side of the stage, in another part of the facility, we see **TITANIA** *who stands over* **COBWEB** *and* **PEASEBLOSSOM** *as they sleep.)*

OBERON & TITANIA.
SOME NIGHTS WHEN HOME CAN BE HARD TO REMEMBER
THE MARK IS A REMINDER OF
TWENTY-THREE THOUSAND THREE HUNDRED AND SIXTY

DAYS SPENT FROM ALL THAT I LOVE

(In silhouette we see all the **ALIENS.***)*

OBERON.   **ALIENS.**

TWENTY-THREE   AH
   THOUSAND THREE
   HUNDRED AND SIXTY
THE TOTAL INCLUDING   AH
   THIS MARK

OBERON & ALIEN WOMEN.   **ALIEN MEN.**

NOW AS THE NIGHT   AH
   COMES I PRAY THAT
   THIS DAY IS
THE LAST WE ARE KEPT IN   AH
   THE DARK

OBERON & ALIENS.

THE LAST WE ARE KEPT IN THE DARK

[MUSIC NO. 14A "SCENE CHANGE"]

Scene Seven

(On the other side of the stage, **AURORA**, **RANDY**, *and* **ELIOT** *stumble into the hangar where they first set up their experiments. Small army tents have been set up.* **ELIOT** *and* **RANDY** *are still fawning over* **AURORA**.*)*

AURORA. Thank goodness. We found it. We're back where we started.

RANDY. Well done, Aurora!

ELIOT. We were lost without you!

AURORA. Will you please stop? I only kept going because I was trying to get away from you two!

*(***REBECCA*** enters, out of breath.)*

REBECCA. Randy! Slow down! So. Many. Stairs.

(Looks at where she is, sudden change.)

Oh, we're here.

AURORA. I need to work on my project.

ELIOT. Yes! The stars, Aurora!

RANDY. Let me help you.

ELIOT. This could be very romantic.

RANDY. Teach me everything you know.

REBECCA. Not this again.

AURORA. Can I have some space please?

ELIOT. Step away, knave.

RANDY. No, I was here first.

AURORA. What is going on? An hour ago all you did was make fun of me and now this? Whatever you're doing is not nice. It hurts.

REBECCA. Randy, stop messing with her.

RANDY. Aurora, I would never hurt you.

REBECCA. Randy, are you listening to me?

RANDY. You are a star.

ELIOT. You are celestial.

RANDY. You are more unique than a thumbprint.

ELIOT. I have had eyes for you since you had braces, then after braces, then a retainer.

RANDY. I love you Aurora, and I dare anyone to say I don't.

ELIOT. You don't. I do.

RANDY. Then let's fight.

ELIOT. Yes, let's fight!

REBECCA. Guys, you don't fight! You're nerds!

ELIOT. Afraid to show some aggression?

RANDY. Perhaps it is time for me to finally unleash my physical prowess.

REBECCA. Hold it. How is it possible that in one day MY boyfriend is suddenly in love with YOU?

AURORA. I don't know. I have nothing to do with it.

REBECCA. Have you been seeing each other behind my back? Why would you take Randy? There are plenty of geeks to go around!

AURORA. I'm not trying to get with Randy!

REBECCA. Or is this all a trick, a mind game so I mess up my presentation and you get to be the star! You're all conspiring against me AND YOU'RE THE MASTERMIND BEHIND IT!

AURORA. I'm not doing anything!

REBECCA. Well, you're doing something! He won't even look at me!

AURORA. I'm zipping up this tent and not coming out until the morning.

RANDY & ELIOT. But the stars, Aurora!

AURORA. I need to be alone. Even if that means I have nothing to present tomorrow. Goodnight all of you crazy people.

ELIOT. I will sleep outside your door. Nothing shall harm you in your slumber.

RANDY. I will be your sentinel. Nothing shall hinder your well-deserved rest.

AURORA. Ugh! Go away!

REBECCA. Both of you. Go to bed. Sleep this off. You better come to your senses by the morning, Randy.

> (**REBECCA** *and* **AURORA** *enter their tents.* **RANDY** *and* **ELIOT** *sit back to back outside* **AURORA**'s *tent. Inside* **REBECCA**'s *tent.*)

[MUSIC NO. 15 "DREAMLAND"]

I'm amazed and don't know what to say.

THIS WAS SUPPOSED TO BE EASY
THIS WAS SUPPOSED TO BE FUN
WITH MEDIA ATTENTION
PLUS A PHOTO-OP WITH AN AIR FORCE COLONEL
THEN SOMEHOW I LOST RANDY
AND THEN LOST EV'RYONE
BEYOND MY COMPREHENSION
THOUGH I TRY TO KEEP MY THOUGHTS INTERNAL
I AM SO UPSET
I HAVE TO SIT AND JOURNAL

> *(She sits and writes furiously.)*

THIS IS NOT AT ALL HOW I THOUGHT THIS WOULD ROLL
SOMEHOW IN AN HOUR I RELINQUISHED ALL CONTROL
I'VE NEVER BEEN THE LOWEST ON THE TOTEM POLE
THANKS DREAMLAND
THANK YOU DREAMLAND

YESTERDAY I SWORE I HAD IT IN THE BAG
GET TO PICK A COLLEGE WITH A PRICIER PRICE TAG
NOW SUDDENLY I'VE STUMBLED ON A GIANT SNAG
CALLED DREAMLAND
IT'S CALLED DREAMLAND

DREAMLAND YOU BIG TIN CAN IN THE DESERT
I'M NOT THE ONE WHO NORMALLY GETS HURT
I HAD A DREAM, AND DREAMLAND YOU KILLED IT
MY CUP WAS FULL AND DREAMLAND YOU SPILLED IT OUT
BUT I WON'T POUT
OR CRY OR SHOUT
MY INK RAN OUT!

(She digs in her backpack, removes:)

Second pen!

(She continues journaling.)

WHERE DID IT GO WRONG AND TELL ME WHO'S IN
    CHARGE
I WAS ONCE THE LEADER OF THE NERD COMMUNITY AT
    LARGE
NOW I'M DUMPED AND LEFT FOR DEAD IN A TOP-SECRET
    BARGE
CALLED DREAMLAND
IT'S CALLED DREAMLAND

INSIDE A PLANE MY LIFE TRAVELS FASTER
SPEEDING THROUGH HIGH SCHOOL, FLEEING DISASTER
DON'T TRY TO STOP MY FORWARD MOMENTUM
SHOW ME YOUR AIRCRAFT, I'LL DOCUMENT 'EM ALL
I'LL SIT AND SCRAWL
I WON'T FREEFALL
I'LL SHOW THEM ALL!

*(In pools of light, each of the **HONOR STUDENT**'s voice their inner thoughts and fears.)*

ELIOT.
DREAMLAND YOU DROPPED ME RIGHT IN THE ACTION

RANDY.
THIS IS A DIFF'RENT KIND OF ATTRACTION

AURORA.
YOU'RE LIKE A WILDFIRE SPREADING AND SPREADING

HONOR STUDENTS.
WHAT SHOULD I DO AND WHERE AM I HEADING?
AT DREAMLAND
DREAMLAND
DREAMLAND!

End of Act I

ACT II

Scene Eight

[MUSIC NO. 15A "ENTR'ACTE"]

(The next morning. **NEW DAWN** *is rehearsing a new song on the presentation stage.* **RASMUSSON** *watches,* **SNYDER** *is now part of the group. He naturally sticks out because he is older, but mostly because he tries to steal the spotlight at every opportunity.)*

[MUSIC NO. 16 "TOTALLY SAFE"]

NEW DAWN.
THIS PLACE IS
TOTALLY SAFE
A LAND OF DREAMS
TOTALLY SAFE
UNDER THE STARS AND STRIPES
TOTALLY SAFE
NO TOXIC SPILLS
SO BRING YOUR KIDS AND
SPEND THE NIGHT!

*(***SNYDER*** starts to sing over the other students, taking solos where there shouldn't be.)*

NEW DAWN & SNYDER.
THIS PLACE IS
TOTALLY SAFE!
SNYDER.
WITH CLEAN BATHROOMS!

NEW DAWN & SNYDER.
> TOTALLY SAFE

SNYDER.
> GO ON AND BOOK YOUR FLIGHT!

NEW DAWN.
> TOTALLY SAFE!

SNYDER.
> NO ALIENS!

NEW DAWN & SNYDER.
> NO ALIENS
> OH YES, YOU HEARD RIGHT!

NEW DAWN & SNYDER.
> THERE ARE NO ALIENS!
> NO, NO ALIENS
> THERE ARE NO ALIENS, NO!
> NO! NO! NO!

NEW DAWN.	**SNYDER.**
THERE ARE NO ALIENS!	NO ALIENS!
NO, NO ALIENS	
THERE ARE NO ALIENS, NO!	
NO! NO! NO!	
THERE ARE NO ALIENS!	THERE ARE NO ALIENS!
NO, NO ALIENS!	THERE ARE NO ALIENS!
THERE ARE NO ALIENS!	THERE ARE NO ALIENS!
N-O!	

> (**SNYDER** *pushes a few people over to make it down center by the button of the number. He strikes a pose, really loving himself.* **RASMUSSON** *approaches the group.*)

RASMUSSON. Amazing! Non-controversial. Approved by bureaucracy. You wrote that overnight?

QUINN. And rehearsed it.

RASMUSSON. That's real music. Keep up the good work, soldiers.

> (*He exits.*)

SNYDER. That was marvelous. I haven't felt this alive in a long time. I feel like you guys are really on to something with this.

(**SCOTT** *is quietly fuming,* **QUINN** *approaches.*)

QUINN. Scott, are you alright?

SCOTT. What are we gonna do?

SNYDER. I think the song is great.

SCOTT. It's not the song.

QUINN. Nope.

SNYDER. Were you thinking perhaps I should come in a little earlier in the number?

QUINN & SCOTT. No.

SNYDER. Well if you're open to critique. I do have a few thoughts.

SCOTT. Oh do you.

SNYDER. I'm thinking the tempo could be a bit brighter, and perhaps the choreography at the top could be a little sharper. It's less a note about the steps, and more about the execution. I'm happy to show the company how I think it should go.

QUINN. I'm sure they'll get it. It's a rehearsal, we don't present until this evening.

SNYDER. Of course, but in the spirit of "workshop," I have a few thoughts about the harmonic progression, and should I be on the melody for more of the song? I do have a three-octave range. Let me help you take this to the next level. Shape this song around my presence. Use me.

SCOTT. That gives me an idea.

SNYDER. Not surprised. Brilliance fuels brilliance.

SCOTT. We do need to showcase your presence. And I agree the story is not being told correctly yet.

SNYDER. Yes, perhaps after the chorus you could vamp and I could present myself as a historian, do a little soft-shoe whilst regaling the audience with fun facts about the base.

SCOTT. No, I have a better role for you.

SNYDER. I'm listening.

SCOTT. Rasmusson said it's crucial the public knows there are no aliens here. But we're missing a visual component that compliments the storytelling.

SNYDER. Go on.

SCOTT. Imagine, as New Dawn sings "No aliens, no aliens" they physically remove an alien threat from the stage, showing the world there is nothing to be scared of.

QUINN. We need an imposing alien threat.

SNYDER. I could play that alien.

SCOTT. Yes.

SNYDER. I could also play the group pushing him away.

QUINN. No. We need you as the ALIEN. Singular imposing figure, the embodiment of mythology and conspiracy.

SCOTT. We even have a costume for you.

SNYDER. Take me to it. (*Addressing the* **SHOW CHOIR**.) Dear friends, the next time you see me, I will be: ALIEN. Unrecognizable in appearance, voice, and mannerisms. Prepare to be amazed.

> (**SCOTT** *and* **QUINN** *lead* **SNYDER** *offstage.*)

QUINN. Take five everyone.

> (*On the other side of the stage we see* **TITANIA**, **PEASEBLOSSOM**, *and* **COBWEB** *who have been watching from a distance.* **PUCK** *enters.*)

PUCK. How goes it, Titania?

TITANIA. I've never seen anything like it. It's certainly not the twist or the mashed potato, but it does have a certain panache. We must start a show choir upon our return home.

PUCK. Do you need any help?

TITANIA. No. I am simply waiting for my moment to get a closer look...at that.

PUCK. A launchpad!

TITANIA. It was erected this morning. The humans call it a stage, but yes. It looks perfect. I haven't been able to get the precise dimensions yet. This group of entertainers refuse to leave it. Even when they take a break, they sit on it. I hope it's not made of magnets. Update on your progress?

PUCK. The humans are sound asleep. I told the others to keep an eye on them.

TITANIA. Will the earthlings be of any use to us?

PUCK. It's possible. There are a few obstacles in the way. But I'm working on it.

TITANIA. And the distraction?

PUCK. Well, that's what I'm working on. You see I made these special glasses that allow humans to see us, but they're not working properly yet.

TITANIA. I told you to forget about those.

PUCK. But –

TITANIA. We don't have time for this! The launchpad has been found! Give me those!

*(She rips them from **PUCK**'s hands.)*

PUCK. No! I'm going to try and fix them.

TITANIA. You are jeopardizing this entire mission! We are all depending on you!

PUCK. But –

TITANIA. Return to them immediately! Think of a distraction! Go foolish Puck. Go!

*(**PUCK** exits. **SCOTT** and **QUINN** reenter.)*

QUINN. OK Snyder, don't come out until we cue you.

SNYDER. *(Offstage.)* Fellow practitioners of art and song, do not fear what you are about to see. For it is only I, Snyder, your intrepid caretaker, playing the role of ALIEN. If at any time my performance proves too convincing, I will remove the mask – ugh. I think it's stuck. Scott, Quinn, can you give me a hand here?

SCOTT. No, the mask is fastened to the costume.

SNYDER. *(Offstage.)* Well can you unfasten it?

QUINN. You'd have to take the whole thing off, let's rehearse the number once first.

SCOTT. Places for the top of the song.

SNYDER. Here I come!

QUINN. No, wait for the music.

SNYDER. *(Offstage.)* Will people recognize me if I have the head on? Perhaps there is a moment where I can reveal myself?

SCOTT. Sweet Auntie Sondheim, just start the song!

QUINN. Five, six, seven, eight!

[MUSIC NO. 17 "AURORA (REPRISE)"]

(The intro to "Totally Safe" begins.)

SNYDER. *(Offstage.)* Enter ALIEN –

QUINN. Not yet!

(Focus shifts to **TITANIA** *who is examining* **PUCK***'s glasses.)*

TITANIA. These glasses do look remarkable. Really a fine bit of engineering.

(She puts them on.)

SCOTT. Now Snyder, now!

*(***TITANIA*** *looks through the glasses and sees* **SNYDER** *enter in all his* **ALIEN** *glory. The music changes abruptly.* **TITANIA** *is in love.)*

(As **TITANIA** *sings she slowly approaches* **SNYDER**. **NEW DAWN** *continues the "Totally Safe Dance," pushing* **SNYDER** *around the stage. The mask and costume is a bit tight on him, he has a hard time maneuvering, seeing, and speaking.)*

TITANIA.
   I CAN'T BELIEVE IT

HAVE I SEEN YOU BEFORE?
YOU'RE UNLIKE THE OTHERS
WITH A FACE I ADORE

YOUR BULBOUS EYEBALLS WHISPER
NO NEED TO BE WARY
YOUR SKIN IS SO SHINY
YOUR HEAD EXTRAORDINARY!
LET'S MARRY. LET'S MARRY!

> (**TITANIA** *pulls* **SNYDER** *off the stage,* **COBWEB** *and* **PEASEBLOSSOM** *follow.*)

SNYDER. Who's pulling me? Where are we going?

TITANIA.
LET'S MARRY. LET'S MARRY!

SNYDER. I can't see anything. Where are you taking me?

> (**NEW DAWN** *finishes the song and poses.*)

NEW DAWN.
N-O!

> (**TITANIA** *slams the door as the music buttons.*)

[MUSIC NO. 17A "SCENE CHANGE"]

Scene Nine

*(Late morning at the **HONOR STUDENTS'** campsite. **RANDY** and **ELIOT** sleep outside of **AURORA**'s tent. **MOTH** and **MUSTARDSEED** keep watch from afar. Slowly and quietly, **AURORA** unzips her tent. As she cautiously stretches her head out of the opening, **RANDY** springs to life.)*

RANDY. Good morning, princess.

AURORA. Oh no.

RANDY. Good morning, my *queen*?

AURORA. Randy, I know you like Rebecca, and the more you do this, the madder she's gonna get, and she's like the closest thing I have to a female friendship at the moment, which is not saying much.

RANDY. Aurora, I only have eyes for you. Rebecca is a thing of the past. She was merely a stepping stone to the relationship I really want. The astronomer, with the cosmos in her eyes.

*(**ELIOT** wakes up.)*

ELIOT. Oh Aurora! Goddess, nymph, perfect, divine. With celestial light your eyes doth shine.

AURORA. Too late, your other homey Romeo already tried to woo me with space imagery. Give it up guys, I don't know why you're doing this. You BOTH like Rebecca. Randy, you hang on her every word. You literally hang ON her. Eliot, every once in a while, I feel like we're connecting, but then she walks by and it's like I'm not even there.

*(**REBECCA** unzips her tent, and crosses to **RANDY**, putting her arms around him.)*

REBECCA. Randy! Good morning. How are you feeling baby bear? Have you come to your senses?

RANDY. *(Brushing her aside.)* Please, I am trying to talk to Aurora, and having another woman in the way is not helping matters.

REBECCA. You've got to be kidding me! Come on, let's go find some breakfast just me and you. You can help me with my presentation after.

RANDY. No.

REBECCA. Randy come here.

RANDY. No.

REBECCA. Randy! Enough is enough. You are my boyfriend and you do as I say. In fact, you are very good at it. Now come here.

RANDY. NO! *(Turning on* **REBECCA**.*)* Why did I waste so much of post-puberty on you?

REBECCA. Excuse me?

RANDY. These are months I can't get back! Find another guy to hold the end of your tape measure.

[MUSIC NO. 18 "KODIAK"]

REBECCA. How dare you!

RANDY. *(Spoken in rhythm.)*
   STOP

ELIOT. Don't get him mad, he'll start speaking in verse.

REBECCA. Randy let's talk about this.

RANDY. *(Spoken in rhythm.)*
   I SAID STOP

REBECCA. Calm down and listen to me!

RANDY. *(Spoken in rhythm.)*
   NO! THAT WAS THE LAST TIME
   YOU GET THE LAST WORD IN
   GO HOME, SHOW'S OVER
   I'M CLOSING THE CURTAIN
   YOU'RE NOTHING BUT A BURDEN
   AND YOU TOOK MY SELF-RESPECT
   WALKING ME AROUND
   LIKE THERE'S A LEASH AROUND MY NECK

TWENTY-FOUR HOURS
WITH A GEIGER COUNTER COUNTING
GAMMA RAYS AND BETA PARTICLES
THAT WERE AMOUNTING TO NOTHING
I FOUND NOTHING! THE COLD HARD FACT IS
YOU'RE THE ONLY THING I'VE FOUND
THAT'S RADIOACTIVE

> (**ELIOT** *picks up the song,* **MUSTARDSEED** *and*
> **MOTH** *join in as well, becoming his invisible*
> *back-up dancers.)*

ELIOT.	**MOTH & MUSTARDSEED.**
REBECCA	REBECCA
YOU GOT HIM	
AGITATED	AGITATED
SORRY THAT YOU	
MUTATED	MUTATED
MORE THAN A	
TEENAGE NINJA TURTLE	TEENAGE NINJA TURTLE
REBECCA, TEN FEET AWAY	
SHE'S GLOWING	SHE'S GLOWING
DON'T TRY TO STAY	
HE'S GOING	HE'S GOING
DUMPING YOU IS	
HIS FINAL HURDLE	HIS FINAL HURDLE

RANDY. *(Spoken in rhythm.)*
YOU TOOK MY SELF-RESPECT, REBECCA
SEE THE WRECK YOU MADE OF ME?
I'M MAD AS HECK REBECCA
SHOW A SPECK OF HUMAN DECENCY
IT'S SO ABSURD, HAVE YOU NOT HEARD
A WORD THAT I'VE SAID RECENTLY?
I'VE SET MY GEIGER COUNTER
TO A MORE ATTRACTIVE FREQUENCY

RANDY, ELIOT, MOTH & MUSTARDSEED.
OH!

RANDY. *(Spoken in rhythm.)*
AURORA'S STRONG AND MAKES ME FEEL INVINCIBLE
IS SOMETHING WRONG?
GO RUN AND TELL THE PRINCIPAL
THE LEASH IS OFF MY NECK REBECCA
AND THERE'S NO GOING BACK
YOUR LITTLE BABY BEAR IS NOW A KODIAK!

ELIOT.	**MOTH & MUSTARDSEED.**
A BIG BEAR	A BIG BEAR
LOOKING FOR	
DIFF'RENT HONEY	DIFF'RENT HONEY
TRUST ME, THIS ISN'T	
FUNNY	FUNNY
HE'S MUCH MORE THAN	
YOUR ARM CANDY	YOUR ARM CANDY
A BIG BEAR	
HE'S DOWN TO EARTH AND	
WORTH IT	WORTH IT
JUST A BIT	
INTROVERTED	INTROVERTED
EV'RYONE WANTS	
A PIECE OF RANDY	A PIECE OF RANDY

RANDY. *(Spoken in rhythm.)*
TICK TOCK TICK TOCK LOOK AT THE CLOCK IT'S
DEPARTURE TIME REBECCA SO HOP INTO YOUR COCKPIT
NOTHING GOOD COMES OUT OF BEING SO CODEPENDENT
DO YOU WANT A COPILOT?
NAH, YOU WANNA FLIGHT ATTENDANT

I'M FREE TO BE THE GUY I WANNA BE
THERE'S YOU AND I, BUT THERE IS NO WE
I GOT THE KEY YOU SEE, YOU'RE NO LONGER MY JAILER
WE'RE BREAKING UP REBECCA. TOSS ME MY INHALER

> (**ELIOT** *does so. He takes a big drag. The song*
> *buttons.* **MOTH** *and* **MUSTARDSEED** *return to*
> *their stakeout position.*)

REBECCA. Fine. If that's the way you want it. I don't need you. I don't need any of you. I'm gonna destroy you all with my presentation. So good luck.

(*The* **GUYS** *immediately turn towards* **AURORA**.)

RANDY & ELIOT. Aurora!

AURORA. Oh, no. You two stay away from me. I command it.

RANDY. Can I help with your presentation, Aurora?

ELIOT. What do you need?

AURORA. Look, it's going to be a very long day, and if your feelings are real, I'm wondering if you could do one tiny thing for me.

ELIOT & RANDY. Anything! Jinx! Break up with Aurora! Never! Darn it!

AURORA. No. Stop. YOU HAVE TO STOP. If you really want to make me happy, go and get your experiments ready to present. Go be the fabulous nerds you are.

RANDY. If you say so.

ELIOT. What he said, but with more understanding and sincerity.

(**REBECCA** *groans.*)

AURORA. Thank you. Now get to work!

[MUSIC NO. 18A "SCENE CHANGE"]

Scene Ten

(TITANIA and her MINIONS lead SNYDER into a breakroom. He is still wearing his ALIEN head, which he cannot take off without assistance.)

TITANIA. Sit him down. Make him comfortable. My, how my love grows for him at such an astonishing speed.

PEASEBLOSSOM & COBWEB. We shall tend to his every need.

SNYDER. Pretty sure I'm hallucinating, not a lot of air in here, but I'll go with it.

TITANIA. If only he could hear my words to understand my devotion to him.

SNYDER. I can't see you, I can't hear you, but I feel your touch, I know you're there.

TITANIA. Massage his sleek smooth head, while I kiss his bulbous eyes.

SNYDER. Oh. That's. Nice. How many hands do you have?

TITANIA. Ha ha. What a jokester. Fetch him a snack.

SNYDER. Perhaps you could help me remove my head?

TITANIA. Remove his head! I could be entertained by this rogue all day. Ha ha.

(PEASEBLOSSOM puts a candy bar into his mouth hole.)

SNYDER. Oh, thank you. I'm starving.

TITANIA. Starving! Poor thing. Fill his mouth with salt and sweets!

PEASEBLOSSOM & COBWEB. We shall let him rest his yapper, and lie him down in bed of candy wrapper.

[MUSIC NO. 19 "SWEET DREAMS"]

(TITANIA and MINIONS recline SNYDER on a break room chair. They raid the vending machine and delicately shove candy into the mouth-hole of SNYDER's alien mask. Perhaps

at some point in the song, we "see" what
SNYDER *"sees:" a room of floating snacks.)*

OFFSTAGE VOICES.
DORITOS, ROLOS
SNICKERS, CHEETOS
FAMOUS AMOS
TWIZZLERS, FRITOS

PEASEBLOSSOM & COBWEB.   **TITANIA.**
DORITOS, ROLOS   HAVE SWEET DREAMS!
SNICKERS, CHEETOS
FAMOUS AMOS   SWEET DREAMS!
TWIZZLERS, FRITOS

TITANIA.
I HAVE NOT SEEN YOU BLINK YET
GO ON, REST YOUR EYES
LET TIME TICK AWAY
THIS ONE SATISFIES
DON'T THINK OF THE CLOCK LET
YOUR MIND BE ON CHOC'LATE
HAVE SWEET DREAMS!
SWEET DREAMS!

(They insert a Snickers into the hole.)

SNYDER. Floating snacks. Definitely hallucinating.

TITANIA.
THERE'S NO WRONG WAY TO EAT IT
WHEN YOU'RE IN DREAMLAND

(Shove a Reese's peanut butter cup.)

THIS MELTS IN YOUR MOUTH
AND NOT IN YOUR HAND

(Shove M&Ms – you get the picture...)

RELAX, LET YOUR BRAIN GO
AND COME TASTE THE RAINBOW
HAVE SWEET DREAMS
SWEET DREAMS!

SNYDER. Would you mind unwrapping things first?

(They sing and dance and unwrap the candies and pour them all into his mask.)

PEASEBLOSSOM & COBWEB. *(Sung as sweetly as possible. Offstage.)*
DORITOS, ROLOS
SNICKERS, CHEETOS
FAMOUS AMOS
TWIZZLERS, FRITOS
SMARTIES, CHEEZ-ITS
REESE'S PIECES

SNYDER. *(As his mask fills with candy.)*
MOTHER MARY
BABY JESUS!

TITANIA, PEASEBLOSSOM, & COBWEB.
SWEET DREAMS!
SWEET DREAMS!

TITANIA.
YOU MIGHT FEEL LIKE A NUT
AND SOMETIMES YOU MIGHT NOT
BUT I HAVE THE TREATS
TO SWEETEN THE POT
I HAVE TO STRIKE NOW
WHILE THE TAMALES ARE HOT
TAKE UP THESE RED VINES
AND LET'S TIE THE KNOT
MY SWEET DREAM!
SWEET DREAM
SWEET DREAM!

> *(**TITANIA** gets on one knee and slides a ring pop on **SNYDER**'s finger. **PUCK** enters, interrupting the snack bacchanal.)*

PUCK. Titania, Cobweb! Peaseblossom! I had an epiphany! Not about the distraction, but I think I know how to fix the glasses, have you seen them?

> *(He sees **TITANIA** wearing the glasses doting on **SNYDER**.)*

Oh. No.

TITANIA. Meet my husband!

PUCK. We don't have time for that right now, drop the snacks and come on!

> (**PUCK** *takes the glasses off her and pulls her away from* **SNYDER**.)

TITANIA. My love!

> (**PUCK** *drags her out,* **COBWEB** *and* **PEASEBLOSSOM** *follow behind, dropping whatever snacks they had been dancing around the room with, startling* **SNYDER**.)

SNYDER. Hello? Hello? That was most peculiar. Well, every life experience is future cabaret material. Break time's over. Now, to conquer the stage!

> (*The "Sweet Dreams" music swells as he exits the breakroom.*)

[MUSIC NO. 19A "SCENE CHANGE"]

Scene Eleven

(The **HONOR STUDENTS**' *bunker.* **REBECCA** *stands in a corner, working on her presentation.* **AURORA** *sits in another corner, flanked by* **RANDY** *and* **ELIOT**. **MUSTARDSEED** *and* **MOTH** *continue to spy from afar.)*

REBECCA. Hello, I am Rebecca Wilson. Senior at Las Vegas Prep School. Licensed pilot with an encyclopedic knowledge of aircraft –

*(***PRINCIPAL WILSON** *enters.)*

PRINCIPAL WILSON. Hello students. How did your experiments go? Are you ready to present?

REBECCA. Mom! Where have you been?

PRINCIPAL WILSON. In my quarters. You said to give you space.

*(***REBECCA** *runs into her mother's arms.)*

REBECCA. Don't ever do that again.

*(***PRINCIPAL WILSON** *smiles.* **COL. RASMUSSON**, **MELISSA SIMMS**, *and* **CAMERA OPERATOR** *enter.)*

RASMUSSON. Alright, scientists, who's ready to pronounce this place alien-free and win that scholarship?

MELISSA. I'm looking for The. Best. Story. And visual aids are always a plus.

REBECCA. I'll go.

MELISSA. Oh. What about that kid with the weather balloon?

ELIOT. I'm prepared, but would prefer to give my slot to Aurora.

RANDY. Me too!

AURORA. I don't have anything to present...

REBECCA. Then I win!

RASMUSSON. This seems unlike any of you. You were all chomping at the bit.

PRINCIPAL WILSON. Maybe they're camera shy.

MELISSA. Really? Yesterday he was trying to jump in my shot.

REBECCA. People change.

AURORA. Randy, Eliot, go. Now.

RANDY & ELIOT. Yes, Aurora.

MELISSA. Wonderful. The competition is heating up! Follow me.

> (**MELISSA**, **PRINCIPAL WILSON**, **RASMUSSON**, **REBECCA**, **RANDY**, *and* **ELIOT** *exit as* **PUCK** *enters and approaches* **AURORA**.)

PUCK. All alone. Perfect. Let's see if these work. Third time's a charm.

> (**PUCK** *slips the glasses on* **AURORA**. *With every "BUM" a shock of energy shoots through a different part of* **AURORA***'s body.*)

[MUSIC NO. 20 "AURORA (REPRISE) / CONTACT"]

MOTH & MUSTARDSEED WITH OFFSTAGE ANGELIC VOICES.
BUM BUM BUM BUM
BUM BUM BUM BUM
BUM BUM BUM BUM
BUM!

> (*But this time,* **AURORA** *is not in love. She can see* **PUCK**. *As they sing:* **AURORA** *waves at* **PUCK**. **PUCK** *waves back.* **AURORA** *smiles.* **PUCK** *smiles.* **PUCK** *advances,* **AURORA** *retreats.* **AURORA** *advances,* **PUCK** *retreats, etc.*)

AURORA & PUCK.
IS IT?
ARE YOU?
CAN YOU?
ARE WE?

AURORA.
> HOW DID?

PUCK.
> HOW DID?

AURORA.
> HOW DO

PUCK.
> HOW DO

AURORA.
> YOU FIRST

PUCK.
> YOU FIRST

AURORA & PUCK.
> SORRY
>
> EVEN THOUGH
> I ALWAYS BELIEVED
> NOW I'M SLOW
> ACCEPTING THE FACT
> HERE WE ARE
> WE SOMEHOW ACHIEVED
> CONTACT
>
> THIS IS
> I MUST
> AM I?
> YOU GO

AURORA.
> WHERE DID?

PUCK.
> WHERE DID?

AURORA.
> WERE YOU?

PUCK.
> WERE YOU?

AURORA.
> IS THIS

PUCK.
>   IS THIS
AURORA & PUCK.
>   HELLO?

>   LIKE A DREAM
>   THOUGH I'M WIDE AWAKE
>   TRYING NOT
>   TO OVERREACT
>   NO ONE THOUGHT
>   THAT WE'D EVER MAKE
AURORA.
>   CONTACT
PUCK.
>   CONTACT

>   *(***TITANIA, COBWEB**, *and* **PEASEBLOSSOM** *enter.)*

AURORA.
>   OH
PUCK.
>   OH
AURORA.
>   OH
PUCK.
>   OH
AURORA.
>   OH

PUCK.	**AURORA.**
CONTACT	OH

AURORA.
>   CONTACT
PUCK & AURORA.
>   OH OH OH OH
>   CONTACT
TITANIA. Well done, Puck.

>   *(***AURORA** *turns to see them, as well as* **MOTH**
>   *and* **MUSTARDSEED**.*)*

AURORA. Holy Halley's Comet there's more of you!

PUCK. Yes –

TITANIA. Wait she can hear us as well?

PUCK. Yes. I made some modifications.

AURORA. On what?

PUCK. The glasses you are wearing. They are invisible, like us.

> (**AURORA** *flips the glasses up and down over her eyes, and the* **ALIENS** *disappear and reappear.)*

AURORA. I have so many questions!

PUCK. Me too. You go first.

AURORA. No, you go first.

PUCK. Do you know Elvis?

AURORA. Elvis? I'm sorry, but he's dead.

PUCK. *Is* he?

TITANIA. Do you have a transistor radio we could borrow?

AURORA. I have this?

> *(She holds up her cell phone.* **PUCK** *grabs it.)*

PUCK. Thank you.

AURORA. Oh, I didn't mean you could keep it, but...okay sure. How am I seeing you? Am I the only one who can see you? How long have you been here?

TITANIA. Shhh. Quiet earthling. Here is what you need to know.

> (**TITANIA** *approaches* **AURORA** *and puts her forehead to hers. She cups her hands over her ears and whispers an incantation. Weird SFX. It's a mind-meld of sorts.* **AURORA** *now has full knowledge of the* **ALIENS**' *plans.)*

AURORA. Whoa. You've been here over sixty years?

TITANIA. Yes.

AURORA. That's horrible. We have to get you home. Your ship has been disassembled, correct?

TITANIA. Yes.

AURORA. And you can reassemble it in three minutes?

TITANIA. We have been practicing for quite a long time.

PUCK. But we have to get the parts above ground –

TITANIA. And to the launchpad.

AURORA. Where's the launchpad?

TITANIA. Over there –

AURORA. The stage! That's in broad daylight, right in front of a television crew. If you're invisible to everyone else, you can't move the pieces up there, they'll look like they're floating!

PUCK. We need a distraction.

TITANIA. Who's out there that can look like they are doing the work, while we actually assemble it?

AURORA. The show choir!

TITANIA. They are quite good, especially the one with the giant head and unblinking eyes.

AURORA. We'll convince them to make their performance about assembling a ship. Your crew can do the real work while New Dawn entertains. No one will know.

PUCK. I knew she was special.

> (**PRINCIPAL WILSON, MELISSA SIMMS, REBECCA, RANDY,** *and* **ELIOT** *re-enter.*)

REBECCA. Aurora, guess who'll be representing Las Vegas Prep on the news tonight?

AURORA. Congratulations. You deserve it.

MELISSA. Not the most exciting of projects, but better than nothing. The other two only talked about you.

PRINCIPAL WILSON. I'm going to tell Colonel Rasmusson the good news. Presentation's in an hour! See you soon.

MELISSA. *(To* **REBECCA**.*)* Keep rehearsing, say it again and again, and like I said, if you can scrounge up a visual aid it would help.

> (*They exit.* **AURORA** *tentatively approaches* **REBECCA**.*)*

AURORA. Congrats Rebecca, you're gonna be amazing.

REBECCA. Yes, the excitement in the room is palpable.

AURORA. I know we haven't been getting along all that well. But I swear I come in peace.

REBECCA. Good one.

AURORA. I might have an idea for the coolest, biggest visual aid in the history of science projects. Remember that Russian spy plane we found underground? What if I –

(**AURORA** *whispers in her ear.*)

REBECCA. You can do that?

AURORA. Not by myself. We're all going to help you. We just might need to tweak your speech a bit. Mind if I have a look?

REBECCA. Be my guest.

AURORA. I'll just make a few edits. You, take the map, I'll meet you down there once I find New Dawn. Randy, Eliot, go with Rebecca.

RANDY & ELIOT. As you wish.

REBECCA. Hey, Aurora. Thanks.

(*They head off.*)

TITANIA. You are very clever earthling.

AURORA. We're going to get you home.

PUCK. You know, you could come with us if you want.

AURORA. I'll think about it.

[MUSIC NO. 20A "SCENE CHANGE"]

Scene Twelve

[MUSIC NO. 21 "ACTION NEWS JINGLE (REPRISE)"]

(Lights rise on **NEW DAWN**'s *stage, moments before the presentation begins.* **MELISSA SIMMS** *prepares to go live.)*

VOICEOVER.
ACTION NEWS. CHANNEL 9 NEWS!
ACTION! ACTION! SO MUCH ACTION!
ACTION NEWS. CHANNEL 9 NEWS
MELISSA SIMMS REPORTING LIVE!

CAMERA OPERATOR. In five, four, three, (two, one)…

MELISSA. Area 51. Top secret military facility. But not anymore. Twenty-four hours have passed. The grounds have been explored, and we are ready to celebrate the grand opening and declassification of what is now called DREAMLAND. Colonel Rasmusson – thoughts?

RASMUSSON. I'd like to let our students do the talking and vouch for this facility's safety and entertainment value.

MELISSA. Well this reporter is happy to announce that she saw nothing out of the ordinary this weekend.

RASMUSSON. Glad to hear.

MELISSA. I stayed in my air-conditioned barracks and never left, but still I felt totally safe. No aliens.

RASMUSSON. No aliens.

MELISSA. We'll hear from one of our student scientists in a few minutes, but let's kick off this celebration with a performance by Las Vegas Prep School's sensational show choir, New Dawn!

[MUSIC NO. 22 "LAST DAY ON EARTH"]

*(***SCOTT** *and* **QUINN** *take center stage as* **NEW DAWN** *freezes in tableau.)*

SCOTT. Tonight we debut a new song that honors the personnel of Dreamland. Men and women who because of the top secret work they were doing, and the non-disclosures they had to sign, remain faceless and nameless.

QUINN. Tonight as we build something before your very eyes, we salute those brave Americans who worked tirelessly to protect and build something else: the American dream.

> (**NEW DAWN** *in flashy new costumes (with new members* **ELIOT** *and* **RANDY***!) perform as they pull up pieces of the ship onto the stage. They are surrounded by* **ALIENS** *who are doing the actual work, quickly assembling the spaceship.)*

NEW DAWN WOMEN.
> REBUILD, RENEW, RECLAIM, REVIEW
> REFLECT, RESOLVE

NEW DAWN WOMEN & MEN.
> RETURN, RESTART
> TAKE AIM, TAKE CHARGE
> TAKE HOLD, TAKE HEART
> TAKE PRIDE, TAKE IN
> TAKE OFF, TAKE PART

> (*Music continues underneath as* **PUCK** *approaches* **AURORA**.)

PUCK. It's actually working!

AURORA. It wasn't a hard sell. Turns out New Dawn was desperate to find a new number. I said, wanna write a song about building a rocket? And boom.

PUCK. So, do you want to come with us?

AURORA. I think I have too much to learn about this planet before I can go somewhere else.

PUCK. Until next time.

AURORA. I hope so, yes.

PUCK. Keep the glasses. Who knows what else you might see.

AURORA. Thanks.

PUCK. I'll be in touch. I have your number.

AURORA. You actually have my phone.

PUCK. So call me.

AURORA. Oh, hey, is there possibly an antidote for Randy and Eliot?

PUCK. You don't want to be loved?

AURORA. Not like that. Maybe someday, and a little less intensely.

PUCK. I'll take care of it.

> (**PUCK** *maneuvers through* **NEW DAWN**, *and grabs* **RANDY** *and* **ELIOT**. **PUCK** *mind-melds them, time appears to slow down as the music changes.*)

If I have at all offended
Think but this, and all is mended
You have only slumbered here
While strange visions did appear
And my flawed, through fruitful, scheme
Had no more substance than a dream.

> (**RANDY** *and* **ELIOT** *forget they were in love with* **AURORA**. *They stand frozen on stage, unsure how they got there.*)

ELIOT & RANDY. Whoa.

ELIOT. What am I wearing?

RANDY. Where is Rebecca?

QUINN. Get in line suckers or get off the stage!

> (**NEW DAWN** *sings some more as* **RANDY** *and* **ELIOT** *try to keep up.* **PUCK** *jumps onto stage helping assemble the spaceship.*)

NEW DAWN.
THERE ARE NO SHADOWS LEFT, AND NOWHERE TO HIDE

WE WALK TO THE GOLDEN LIGHT GLOWING WITH PRIDE

NEW DAWN WOMEN.

NOTHING TO CONCEAL

NEW DAWN.

WE STAND AND REVEAL

WHAT'S INSIDE

NEW DAWN MEN.

WHAT'S INSIDE

NEW DAWN.

SO WE MAY NEVER KNOW, WHEN OUR COUNTDOWN
STARTS

BUT WE KEPT OUR PROMISES, WE PLAYED OUR PARTS

NEW DAWN WOMEN.

AS OUR PLANET SPINS

NEW DAWN.

IT ENDS AND BEGINS

WITH OUR HEARTS

WITH OUR HEARTS

LIVE LIKE IT'S YOUR LAST DAY ON EARTH

LOVE LIKE IT'S YOUR LAST DAY ON EARTH

EV'RYWHERE YOU LOOK

THERE'S SOMETHING WAITING TO BE KNOWN

TURN OVER THE STONE

AND LIVE LIKE IT'S YOUR LAST DAY ON EARTH

(Variously.)

BUILD A ROAD BRICK BY BRICK, AND FORGE YOUR OWN
WAY

AND SPEAK ALL THE WORDS THAT ARE HARDEST TO SAY

THERE'S A NEW FRONTIER

YOU'RE THE PIONEER

OF TODAY

OF TODAY

LIVE LIKE IT'S YOUR LAST DAY ON EARTH

LOVE LIKE IT'S YOUR LAST DAY ON EARTH

NEW DAWN GROUP #1.	NEW DAWN GROUP #2.
EV'RYWHERE YOU LOOK	LOOK EV'RYWHERE
THERE'S SOMETHING	
WAITING TO BE KNOWN	

NEW DAWN.
TURN OVER THE STONE
AND LIVE LIKE IT'S YOUR LAST DAY ON EARTH!

> *(The ship is now fully assembled, so dance break!* **NEW DAWN** *is unaware they are dancing side by side with* **ALIENS**. *The end of the dance reveals* **REBECCA** *standing at a podium.)*

REBECCA. Hello, I am Rebecca Wilson. Senior at Las Vegas Prep School and licensed pilot with an encyclopedic knowledge of aircraft. I'm guessing ninety-nine point nine percent of this country has never seen the thing towering behind me. It's what you might call an unidentified flying object. But not anymore, I have spent the last day cataloging all of the unique and incredible ships you will encounter on this base, and this one is my favorite.

REBECCA.	NEW DAWN WOMEN.
	(Underneath the speech.)
Something the world has never seen: a Russian Sikorsky-era spy plane.	REBUILD, RENEW RECLAIM, REVIEW REFLECT, RESOLVE
Most likely the only one in existence, or at least in this kind of pristine shape.	**NEW DAWN.** RETURN, RESTART
It is planes like this that are waiting for you here at Dreamland: secret dinosaurs of aeronautic history that will never fly again.	TAKE AIM, TAKE CHARGE

Do yourself a favor and come see first-hand the innovation and breadth of imagination contained at this facility.

TAKE HOLD, TAKE HEART

Dreamland is free of aliens but full of fun.

TAKE PRIDE, TAKE IN

I am honored to announce the conspiracy case closed, and Dreamland officially open!

TAKE OFF, TAKE PART

> (**SNYDER** *enters. He is still wearing the mask and is totally discombobulated. He moves through the show choir like a bull in a china shop.*)

SNYDER. I found you guys! Finally! I love the new song! Where should I go? Where should I stand?

TITANIA. Take his hands and lead him on board!

> (**COBWEB**, **PEASEBLOSSOM**, **MOTH**, *and* **MUSTARDSEED** *pull him onto the ship, as he waves goodbye.*)

SNYDER. *(Notices the rocket ship.)* Oh! Did you build this for me? Of course, grand finale, the alien returns home!

OBERON. Thank you, brave stargazer. We shall see you in the cosmos!

AURORA. Farewell!

NEW DAWN.
SING LIKE IT'S YOUR LAST DAY ON EARTH
DANCE LIKE IT'S YOUR LAST DAY ON EARTH

NEW DAWN GROUP #1.   **NEW DAWN GROUP #2.**
EV'RYWHERE YOU LOOK   LOOK EV'RYWHERE
THERE'S SOMETHING
    WAITING TO BE KNOWN

NEW DAWN.
TURN OVER THE STONE

AND LIVE LIKE IT'S YOUR LAST DAY ON EARTH
LOVE LIKE IT'S YOUR LAST DAY ON EARTH

NEW DAWN GROUP #1.   **NEW DAWN GROUP #2.**
EV'RYWHERE YOU LOOK   LOOK EV'RYWHERE
THERE'S SOMETHING
    WAITING TO BE KNOWN

NEW DAWN.
TURN OVER THE STONE
AND LIVE LIKE IT'S YOUR LAST DAY ON EARTH
LAST DAY ON EARTH
LAST DAY ON EARTH

>(**NEW DAWN** *poses, smiling and panting, with a gleaming rocket ship built behind them. Then a low rumbling. The stage fills with smoke as the spaceship lifts off. It is glorious.)*

MELISSA. *(To* **CAMERA OPERATOR.***)* You got all of that right?

CAMERA OPERATOR. Yup.

MELISSA. It just, lifted off into space.

CAMERA OPERATOR. Fastest thing I've ever seen.

>*(In a frenzy,* **RASMUSSON** *jumps on stage, facing the camera.)*

RASMUSSON. Thank you thank you thank you all! What a finale. Couldn't have planned it better myself. Thanks for a successful weekend and hope to see you all at Dreamland. New Dawn, sing that New Dawn song again!!

SCOTT & QUINN. Costume change!

>*(All of* **NEW DAWN** *rush offstage.* **RASMUSSON** *runs out another way.)*

MELISSA. *(To* **RASMUSSON.***)* Not so fast! *(To* **CAMERA OPERATOR.***)* Follow him! Colonel Rasmusson, was that plane really what the nerd kid said it was? *(Back to* **CAMERA OPERATOR.***)* Come on! We just stumbled on the story of a lifetime!

>*(They exit chasing after* **RASMUSSON.** *As the smoke clears, we see* **REBECCA** *sitting on one*

side of the stage and **AURORA** *on the other.*
PRINCIPAL WILSON *rushes over to* **REBECCA**.)

PRINCIPAL WILSON. Rebecca! There you are! Are you okay?

REBECCA. I'm fine.

PRINCIPAL WILSON. You're not hurt? Is anyone hurt?

REBECCA. I don't think so.

PRINCIPAL WILSON. We are on the next bus out of here, right after I give Colonel Rasmusson a piece of my mind.

(She runs off. **RANDY** *enters.)*

RANDY. Hey baby bear.

REBECCA. Hey.

*(***RANDY*** *kisses her head.)*

Are you talking to me again?

RANDY. When would I not talk to you?

REBECCA. Are you kidding?

RANDY. What do you mean?

REBECCA. I guess I haven't been the greatest girlfriend.

RANDY. Rebecca, you're the smartest, most driven person I've ever met. I learn something new from you every day.

REBECCA. I just made a fool of myself on national television.

RANDY. I thought you were great.

REBECCA. Full-ride or not, what school would accept me after that?

RANDY. What school wouldn't?

REBECCA. Randy.

RANDY. Everyone in the world is going to want more information about what they just saw here, and you're the only person on the planet who measured every inch of that aircraft and has a notebook full of data to prove it. You'll pick your college, your job, and your salary.

REBECCA. I'll only look at schools with the very best geology programs. I'd really like you to come along with me. But only if you want to...

RANDY. That would be great.

REBECCA. Baby bear.

> (**RANDY** *holds* **REBECCA**, *they turn to watch*
> **NEW DAWN**. *On the other side of the stage*
> **ELIOT** *approaches* **AURORA**.)

ELIOT. Hey.

AURORA. Hey.

ELIOT. Is that my...blazer?

AURORA. Oh yeah, sorry.

ELIOT. No no, you look good in it. Aurora, what just happened?

AURORA. It was an alien spacecraft. Full of aliens. And we just sent them home.

ELIOT. Whoa. I don't remember a lot of the last twenty-four hours. It's kind of a blur. In fact the only thing that's really clear in my head is you. It's like I'm seeing you in a different way... You're deep.

AURORA. Yikes.

ELIOT. No, I like it. *(Beat.)* Maybe we can hang out sometime? There's this coffee shop at the top of the Stratosphere Hotel that I love going to whenever there's a storm. You can see the clouds forming from miles away. It's amazing.

AURORA. But it's the desert, it never storms.

ELIOT. It rains two days a month.

AURORA. For someone who loves the weather, you are really in the wrong place.

ELIOT. Maybe we don't wait for a rainstorm. You could take me stargazing?

AURORA. I'd like that.

ELIOT. I want you to teach me everything you know.

AURORA. *(Laughs to herself, then slowly.)* "It is not in the stars to hold our destiny, but in ourselves."

ELIOT. Who said that?

AURORA. I dunno. Shakespeare?

(He offers his hand, she takes it. A triumphant fanfare as **NEW DAWN** *takes the stage in glorious bedazzled costumes.)*

[MUSIC NO. 23 "FINALE"]

NEW DAWN.

AAH!
NOW THE STARS HAVE ALL DESCENDED
AND OUR YESTERDAYS ARE DONE
THOUGH OUR JOURNEY'S OPEN-ENDED
WE STARE OUT AT THE SUN!
(Variously.) OH, I CAN SEE IT'S YOU AND ME
OH OH
(Together.) A NEW DAWN

ALL.

(Variously.) NOW WE CAN, NOW WE CAN
NOW WE CAN WAKE UP
NOW WE CAN, NOW WE CAN
TAKE UP OUR SONG
NOW WE CAN, NOW WE CAN
(Together.) FINALLY SHAKE UP THE RULES
AND MAKE RIGHT OUR WRONGS
OH OH
OH OH

MEN.

A NEW DAWN

MEN & WOMEN.

A NEW DAWN

MEN.

A NEW DAWN

MEN & WOMEN.

A NEW DAWN

[MUSIC NO. 24 "BOWS"]

End of Play

Milton Keynes UK
Ingram Content Group UK Ltd.
UKHW032034130224
437791UK00016B/1116

9 780573 708428